AMIRANDA

Enjoy the Adventure!!!

AMIRANDA

PRINCESS AMIRANDA AND THE TALE OF THE DECIDUOUS FOREST

JOHN P. ADAMO

Legwork Team Publishing
New York

Legwork Team Publishing
80 Davids Drive, Suite One
Hauppauge, NY 11788
www.legworkteam.com
Phone: 631-944-6511

ISBN: 978-1-935905-41-7 (sc)

First Edition 05/08/2012

Printed in the United States of America
This book is printed on acid-free paper

Designed by Vaiva Ulenas-Boertje

*This book is dedicated to
my own grandmother, "Nana,"
who brought our family together
with both her food and her love.*

When will the sky clear?
When will the rain disappear?
Don't let go of your dreams;
Don't let go.
—John Adamo

Contents

The following story is purely a fairy tale....

Prelude

Peace had always reigned over the small town of Luxing. There, nestled high upon a hill overlooking the plains and forest below, lived a king and his royal family. The castle in which they lived was both strong and secure. The king held the highest standards for both himself and his family, and he tried to use his power only for the good of the kingdom. After all, he wanted what was best for everyone—especially for his daughter and only child, Princess Amiranda.

Princess Amiranda spent her childhood years preparing for life as a noble, a life for which she was distinctly destined. However, the young princess always had an insatiable urge for learning—learning from the real world around her, the same world from which her father, the king of Luxing, strongly safeguarded her.

From her castle window, Amiranda would gaze at the beautiful countryside below—always watching carefully; always observing everything. Gradually, the princess would realize that she knows very little of the small kingdom over which she would one day reign. Nevertheless, Amiranda would never disobey her father's wishes, especially the one to never enter the mysterious dark forest, which borders their kingdom. That is, until one day when she would have no other choice....

Acknowledgments

I acknowledge the dedicated efforts of Yvonne Kamerling and Janet Yudewitz of Legwork Team Publishing. I extend my gratitude to them and their team of design, editorial, and technical professionals, for transforming my story into the book you hold in your hands.

My heartfelt appreciation also goes out to Elna Gottlieb, who helped me edit parts of this book and transform it from a drawn out screenplay into a working novel, Betsy Stevens for proofreading the first few drafts and revisions, Vaiva Ulenas-Boertje for her help with layout and design, and Nancy Carrasco for final editing as well as encouraging me to complete the novel.

I would also like to thank the people who made the biggest personal impressions on my life, and helped inspire me: My piano teacher Doug Russell, for teaching me how to play piano and write music. My father John Adamo Sr., who worked long, hard hours but still managed to take the time to go fishing, play ball, collect coins, and do other father-son types of things with me. And finally my grandmother, Rose D'Angelo (also known as "Nana"), to whom I am dedicating this book. Rose was a truly incredible person, who literally could make a friend right on the street and then invite them into her house for dinner. Even as cliché as it may sound, she was the glue that held my family together.

Lastly, I would like to thank the wonderful skills and the beautiful illustrations provided by Christopher Donovan, who brought many of my characters to life through his amazing artwork. Christopher has shown the same dedication and attention to detail that I try to place on this work. I am truly grateful for everything he has done to make this story truly unique and complete.

Introduction

The Butterfly

One of spring's first leaves is suddenly loosened by a small yet sudden burst of mild wind. The bright green almond-shaped leaf falls like a piece of paper, ever so lightly in the cool, calm breeze. Gently and slowly it settles into the peaceful pond below. The contact of this single tiny leaf causes many small waves to ripple outward in the water—a catalyst for things to soon follow.

A nearby lily pad sails along the sudden current, causing a golden-yellow butterfly perched on top of it to take flight. The colorful butterfly playfully flutters along, flying through the tall green grass and the wild golden-brown willows that surround the pond. Her bright yellow and orange wings sparkle radiantly in the sunshine, displaying quite a beautiful sight. Gracefully, she glides out of the maze of grassland, maneuvering through the brush, darting around low-lying branches, and dodging other flying insects, all without missing a beat.

Heading toward higher ground, the butterfly flutters around almost aimlessly for a moment, and then soars to a window of the nearby castle to rest. As she rests, her delicate wings gently move back and forth together in harmony. In concert, they gracefully open up and close, like a slow but steady rhythmic heartbeat. The colorful image of her own reflection in the glass window quickly catches her own attention.

Looking at her own likeness, the butterfly is unaware that it is her own beauty she sees. Carefully she watches as the golds, yellows, and subtle hints of orange dance on the mirrored panes of glass. Caught up in the kaleidoscope of color, she sits there staring, mesmerized, wondering how this creature before her could be made so beautiful. How odd, she thinks to herself, how someone could show off in such a manner—purposely copying *her own* movements. Surely, if she were that beautiful, she would not do the same.

Quietly, the butterfly's wings become still and her antennae wilt like a flower that has gone days upon days without water. Deeply saddened that she cannot compare to the showy stranger, the butterfly darts off into the crystal-blue sky above, seeking comfort. However, our focus does not follow. The curious happenings occurring within the castle draws our attention closer inside.

Introduction

The Castle

The palace is truly enormous in every sense of the word. By far, it is the biggest, the tallest, and the sturdiest structure within the entire kingdom. It is so large, in fact, that the nearby buildings are dwarfed in comparison. Built stone by stone, it took nearly a thousand men over half a century to create. All of this was done in order to protect the king and his royal family. At first it is hard to see what is inside the castle's dense, solid walls and considerably thick windowpanes; however, slowly and surely, an image comes into view.

Introduction

Surprisingly, the look and feel inside the castle is as vibrant and alive as the wonders of nature which surround it, as one could rightfully imagine. The room is simple yet elegant, placing deep faith in the notion that less is more.

Even though it is one of the smaller rooms at the back end of the castle, the space is by no means small. After all, it is the royal castle's leisure room, a place designed for the members of the royal family to gather, meet, and greet one another. There are several different areas within the quarters where they can relax, entertain, sip tea, and informally talk to one another, although any type of recreation rarely takes place here within the castle's walls. In fact, it has been years since this room has been used for any of these purposes in particular.

A black and white checkerboard of square marble tiles lines the floor of the room, and random splashes of color are placed around for sharp, dynamic contrast. Rich, vibrant colors of gold accent the space, distinctly showing the royalty's prominence. Velvety tones of red and subtle hints of orange complement the regal, plum-colored walls. Hanging down majestically from the ceiling, there are two twenty-four karat solid gold chandeliers. The shimmering crystals of the lights cascade downward, resembling fireworks exploding in the night sky, creating an atmosphere both majestic and intriguing.

On the right side of the room is the room's main entryway. An oversized, arched wooden door emphasizes the castle's royal importance. In fact, it looks more like a drawbridge than any doorway that would be found in a typical house or home. Made of broad, heavy, solid panels of timber, the castle door can be imagined to be at least six inches thick—a door both strong enough and fit enough to protect a fortress such as this.

In one corner of the room, just to the left of the main entryway, is a place to sit and eat small meals. Quite casual by design, there is an island-style kitchen counter for a member of the staff to prepare breakfast, lunch, or a light snack for members of the royal family. In front of the table, perfectly lined up in a row, there are four somewhat typical, yet very stylish, wooden bar stools on which to sit and enjoy a freshly prepared meal. A row of cupboards and cabinets line the back wall, creating a chef's alcove or small nook. Although this layout is far different from the royal castle's much more formal, elegant, and grandiose dining area, still, for a room so large it proves to be both cozy and inviting. There are many spatulas, ladles, cooking wisps, salad strainers, and even a handful of mixers—all of which are highly-polished, neatly draped on hooks, and put proudly on display. As the old saying goes, there is a place for everything. Currently, everything is neatly in its place.

Centered on the main wall, there is one great big window which opens out onto the west, directly facing the countryside. Just below and to one side of the room's main window stands a highly ornate and handcrafted grand piano. The grand-sized piano is made from imperial rosewood and other exotic materials. These materials are only known to be owned and imported by those elite enough to do so. As with everything else, the craftsmanship displayed on the piano is of the highest level known, and the attention to detail is painstakingly meticulous. The light from the early morning sun brightly illuminates the reddish cherry-brown tones of the wood, and shimmers off the ivory-white keys of the majestic instrument, making it appear almost as if it was alive. Like everything else in the room, it is overly polished and pristine.

On the far left side of the room ascends a wide, quarter-turn staircase which spirals upward to the next floor. Made from genuine marble that was all seamlessly joined together, the elegant staircase creates the illusion that it was chiseled out of one solid piece of stone. The staircase is very open and airy, allowing one to see someone coming down or going up, except for the very top stairs, which remain hidden from view.

Just to the left of the main window, a large brass birdcage rests atop a tall brass stand. With the cage door presently left wide open, a bright multicolored parrot sits atop the dome-shaped cage. Playfully the parrot climbs into the cage and hangs upside down by his large talons. He bobs his head up and down, inverted within the cage, only to fly out once again. The colorful bird flies around the room for a minute, swooping around in large roundabout circles, before attempting to alight on the kitchen countertop. It is clear to see that the parrot is fully efficient at flying, but not at landing. With his feathers ruffled, he begins to nudge them gently back into place.

Just then, the castle's fortress-like wooden door opens abruptly....

Chapter 1

The Young Princess

A stately dressed butler properly adorned in elegant black tails hurries into the room. He is medium in height, lean in stature, and has balding gray and silver hair. With his gloved hand, he brushes his fingers through his hair, making sure each one is neatly in place.

"Amiranda, hurry down here!" the proficient butler calls out to her. Although emphatic, he is careful not to shout, as that would be undignified. "Already you are way off your schedule! You know if you're not down here promptly for your piano practice, your father will surely have my hide!"

The butler is hastily running his routine around the castle as he always tries to maintain a rigid schedule. He is fervent as far as his customary duties are concerned and has no time for amusement. Ritualistically, he prepares some sheet music by the piano for Amiranda to play.

Although unseen, a young girl's voice replies politely, "Can't I have breakfast first today, Jove? It's too early to practice, I just woke up." The girl's sweet voice rings clearly from the top of the stairs. She has the kind of voice that resonates in the purest of tones and with the most perfect pitch, yet remains timid and not overpowering.

Reluctantly abiding to the butler's wishes, the young princess slowly makes her way down the grand marble staircase. She is seen first only by her bare feet, and then by the frilled white lace bottom of her long and flowing nightgown, which is neatly hemmed at ankle length. Pitter-pattering at her feet are the paws of her puppy. As always, he moves closely along beside her.

Clumsily the young pup makes his way down the stairs, too small to manage proficiently by himself, although he tries. He constantly trips on Amiranda's toes as she descends the stairway, but she remains diligently careful not to step on her furry and faithful companion. After all, he is her best friend.

Next to be seen of the princess is a small, white ribbon that is centered mid length on her nightgown and neatly sewn onto her dress. Her graceful, long arms lead up to the puffs of the short sleeves on her garment. Her gown is quite typical of any young girl's usual nightwear, although noble and royal she is.

As the princess makes her way down the stairs, her face gradually comes into view. Amiranda is a teenager, yet still somewhat childlike in appearance; she has wavy light-brown hair and a ski-sloped button nose that ripples daintily whenever she smiles. Her countenance shines as she walks into the sunlit room and her beauty always appears to be as natural as the sunshine outdoors. As she makes her way down the staircase, toward the black and white marble tile floor at the bottom of the stairs, her pup, Peatie, trips uncontrollably at her feet.

"Oh Peatie, are you all right?" Amiranda asks, concerned for her devoted companion. The young princess picks up her pup, cupping him in the palm of her hand. Ever protective of him, she carries and cradles him the rest of the way.

Peatie is a brown and white puppy; very small and fragile, he is not unlike a small beagle. He has an adorably cute white face, a small black nose, and a brown-colored patch that circles his left eye. The small pup licks the tip of her nose, causing cute dainty ripples to appear on it.

"Good morning Jove, how are you today?" the princess asks kindly, with a genuine concern for her assistant's well-being.

"Good morning, Amiranda." Jove replies hastily. "And no, you can't have breakfast before your piano lesson or even during your piano lesson for that matter, and I'm quite fine thank you."

The proficient butler begins to prep some kitchen utensils from behind the counter, placing them onto the table. He is always meticulous and neat.

"You know your father has designated a strict schedule in which you must keep," he continues to tell her, reminding her of his civil duties, which the young princess already knows all too well. "Besides, if you do not get enough practice, then you may hit a wrong note during your royal recital. I don't want *that* on my permanent record. After all, you know how the old saying goes, 'the butler did it.'"

Jove's message is stated with the typical mannerism and professionalism of a butler—very straightforward, always to the point, and only stating what needs to be said.

"Oh Jove, you are always being melodramatic," Amiranda points out to him, wishing he could be a little less rigid and a lot more compassionate. Abiding halfheartedly, she begins to sit down at the piano, shuffling through the pages. "For once I want to do what I want to do, when I want to do it," she declares with a hint of mysticism inflected in her voice.

Amiranda opens up and thumbs through her lesson book to appease the butler's wishes as well as her father's. She stares at the sheet music blindly, almost looking right through it. It is as though the pages were not even there. Knowing all of her lessons by heart, they might as well not be there as she can breeze right through them without even looking.

"You know I'll never grow up living like this," she tells him cordially. She is almost pouting, but not quite, as she knows better than to do so.

"That is for you and your parents to decide; I merely enforce their rules. Besides, you know how royalty can be. Someday it will be your turn to enforce your own rules, but for now it is time for us to prepare you for that day."

Jove carefully checks his pocket watch. Looking at the time displayed, he calculates against his usual appointed rounds. Amiranda's tardiness has already put him way behind schedule. Jove lets out a sigh, as this is quite typical of the young princess.

"Now, if you'll excuse me, I have to tend to some other chores for a while," the noble servant says as he closes his watch and puts it away, neatly tucking the chain away to prevent tangling.

The butler opens the main window of the room, letting in the light from the gorgeously bright and sunny day. The warm and fresh spring air comes rushing in, filling the room with the season's beautiful fragrance. It smells just like the roses that are climbing right outside, up along the walls of the castle and almost into the room. The aroma is nearly sweet enough to fully wake Amiranda, herself still somewhat asleep.

"I will be back to check up on you in a jiffy," Jove tells her. The antsy butler then exits the room for Amiranda to practice, as he attends to his other responsibilities. With the exception of her two animal companions, her pup, Peatie, and her parrot, Reynolds, the princess is left all alone.

Immediately upon Jove's departure, the brightly colored parrot squawks, noisily mimicking the butler's words. "In a jiffy! Arrk! In a jiffy! Warrk!" The playful bird flies over to the piano and perches himself on top of the music rack, directly in front of Amiranda. Flamboyantly, he spreads his wings wide open, displaying how truly beautiful and colorful he is. It is obvious that he is trying to get some attention. Then, and even more surprisingly whimsical to Amiranda, he echoes, "The butler did it! Warrk! The butler did it!"

The young princess cannot help to be both amused and perplexed by the parrot's peculiar behavior. It seems that he continually tends to pick up on certain phrases, which he then chooses to utter in order to amuse himself and those around him, but primarily Amiranda. She often wonders where he picks up on these things; and if he actually knows exactly what it is he is saying.

"Oh be quiet, Reynolds," Amiranda exclaims with a slight giggle. "You too can be a bit melodramatic yourself, you know," she tells him. The princess turns to her pup for agreement, "Isn't that right Peatie?"

Amiranda picks up her pup, neatly coils him up into a ball, which perfectly fits in the palm of her hand and presses her nose firmly against his, just the way she so often does. Peatie licks the tip of her nose in agreement and the princess smiles.

Although Reynolds tries his best to pay the two no mind, the reflection of Amiranda holding Peatie can be seen in Reynold's eyes as he watches them. Although the parrot hates to be petted, he still vies for the princess' kindness; he just does so in a different way. Gently, Amiranda places Peatie down on top of the piano.

"Arkk! Mel-o-dramatic! Mel-o-dramatic!" the parrot echoes in reply, as he flies directly back to his cage. Once again he lets himself inside, only to bob himself upside down, strictly for show. It is easy for anyone to see the contest for Amiranda's affection between the frail pup and the showy parrot.

"Sometimes I wonder if you really know what you're saying," Amiranda states, asking herself, or perhaps even the parrot for that matter. It is also plain to see that the princess is in no hurry to begin her practice, as she does her best to procrastinate or postpone it. Her mind starts to wander. For a second she remembers a dream she had last night, but quickly she then forgets, her eyes looking out to the countryside.

"I wonder what life is really like, beyond these walls, outside these doors, and even past this kingdom, beyond the forest," she softly whispers to herself. "If only given the chance, I am certain I could touch the stars and carry a piece of them with me," she says looking up to the sky.

A gentle sigh is heard in the young girl's voice as her mind continues to drift farther and farther away. Her distant dreaming is ever so slight at first, and then grows deeper toward a fantasy world that she only wishes were real. There is a distinguishable look of wonder displayed within her eyes, emanating deep from behind her pupils. It dwells deep within her soul, far within the confines of her mind, a mind that remains unsettled.

Amiranda realizes she knows very little about the real world around her, although that is the one thing everyone is trying their best to prepare her for. Life, as known to her, is clearly defined by the many solid stones which make up the walls that surround her; it is a life of preparing to be a noble.

Focusing her attention to the outside surroundings—first the pond, then the field, and finally the forest beyond, her eyes affix to the same gold-colored butterfly as spoken of before. The unrestrained creature flies about with ease, quietly gliding and tumbling gracefully in the outside air. The princess begins to dream what life would be like if she were flying—peaceful, effortless, free.

"Why, if only I had wings, then I could surely fly like a bird, or even a butterfly," she tells herself. Taking a deep breath, she pauses, still thinking. Finally, she snaps back out of her fantasy world, now faced with reality. Amiranda takes a short breath before she begins to arbitrarily tap on the keys of the piano. It is a routine for her, setting out to improve herself for the sake of her noble family and namely her father, always abiding by *his* wishes.

As Amiranda tinkers with the notes, her mind continues to drift as it often does. It is partly due to her curiosity of life, and partly because of her bright and vivid imagination, as that is the one thing that no one can take away from her. She pays no attention to the sheet music she is supposed to play and begins to play a different tune. Having practiced every day for the past twelve years of her life, the princess is proficient enough at composing her own music at will. Gazing up, looking out the great window that rests just above the top edge of the grand piano, Amiranda continues to daydream.

Playing the notes on the piano one by one, she begins to sing softly out loud to herself, and her two pets ...

If I could fly
I'd surely have wings;
I'd rise to the top
Of anything
If I could fly, if I could fly.

If I could fly
I'd surely have wings;
I'd rise to the top
Of anything.

I'd rise high and soar to the mountains
I'd fly straight and sure to the seas.
I'd live the life I want to be in
And at last have the chance to be free.

If I could fly
I'd soar through the sky;
I'd know all the answers
To who, where, and why.

Is there gold at the end of the rainbow?
Is there someplace that's better for me?
Could I find a world I can live in?
For once I'll hold the key.

If I could fly
I'd surely have wings;
I'd rise to the top
Of anything
If I could, if I would, if I could fly.

Although Amiranda's song starts out very solemn in the beginning, as she continues to sing, both the tune and the melody grow happier, as if the words she was singing were somehow coming true. Somewhere deep within her heart, she truly imagines that they are. Her voice is naturally animated and the young princess sings both sweetly and melodiously. She has an innate talent, which simply cannot be learned.

The princess begins to dance around the room by herself as the song grows more and more cheerful. After a few moments of dancing alone, Amiranda picks up her pup and twirls him around and around while carefully holding him in her arms. She even lightly tosses him up in the air and then softly catches him, which Peatie seems to really enjoy. Her delicate smile radiates from within, joyous in her own fantasy realm.

About halfway through her song, the gold-colored butterfly enters the room, flying in from the great window Jove had opened just moments earlier. Attracted to her melodious voice, the winged creature flutters around the princess effortlessly, dancing around her as she sings. Amiranda carefully places her pup back down on top of the piano and begins to imitate the butterfly's graceful movements.

Whenever Amiranda dances, her movements eloquently mimic the butterfly in flight, as they are very poised and flowing. She copies the fluttering, flapping motions of the butterfly's wings with her long, graceful arms, swaying them back and forth and side to side. The two circle around one another elegantly, both investigating each other as they dance their fanciful ballet.

Without question, it is hard to determine who is more poised—Amiranda herself or the fanciful butterfly. Amiranda imitates her partner's natural motions with ease, smiling graciously the whole time. Cordially, the butterfly returns the compliment, using its irregular and unpredictable flight patterns to accurately portray the princess' emotions. The happier Amiranda is, the more fancifully the butterfly flies. It is an affectionate display of style, warmth, elegance, and beauty.

Fully satisfied with their performance, Amiranda extends her hand out to the butterfly for it to land, which it does. Drawing her arm in closer to her, Amiranda looks at the butterfly as the butterfly looks back at Amiranda. The two are nose-to-nose and face-to-face, almost close enough to touch.

The princess carefully examines the beautiful markings and elegant patterns displayed on the butterfly's colorful wings as they flap ever so slowly in her hand. Amiranda always takes note of the sheer beauty displayed within all of nature, and she marvels at how anyone could fashion such a beautiful creature. How fragile, yet how resilient it must be. She wonders how it is able to travel hundreds upon hundreds of miles alone in the wilderness; yet it appears to be so delicate and frail. Surely, if Amiranda were a delicate creature left alone in the wilderness, she would not fare as well. The butterfly is truly an astonishing creature.

Thoughts and questions like these always intrigue Amiranda. She is wholesome enough to notice many of the intricacies and ironies consistently placed throughout nature, and mindful enough to respect them for what they are. Complete with her examination of the beautiful

winged-creature, the young princess extends her arm outward once again. The butterfly takes flight, exiting out the window from which she came.

At the end of her song, Amiranda repeats the words "If I could fly" over and over again, saying them softer and softer. She sings the words quietly, reverently, as in prayer. Her voice quickly saddens, knowing that her wish could never truly be fulfilled. When the princess finishes her song, there she remains, in the confines of her home, with the same customary rules of aristocracy surrounding her.

"Wouldn't life be just wonderful Peatie," she asks, "if just for a moment we could fly way up and then look down at the world around us?" Peatie lets out a slight yelp, as if in agreement to her hypothetical question.

Despite being faced with reality, there is still a slight glimmer of hope detected in Amiranda's otherwise somber voice. Determined not to falter, once again she picks up Peatie, twirls him around gently cupped in her hands. She is quite happy to have such a wonderful and friendly companion.

Amiranda is vibrant in both movement and in character, and yet at the same time, she is quite "down-to-earth." She knows the difference between reality and fantasy, but she still often tries to bridge the gap between the two—a thing that many adults have strictly taught themselves not to do.

After a moment's pause, the princess' mind slowly transitions itself back to reality. She never has a loss of her senses, she is just bursting with imagination. She is also puzzled by the way things are, and the way things ought to be. All is quiet for a moment, but not for long.

"Wark! Mel-o-dramatic! Arrk! Mel-ooo-dramatic!" the parrot squawks as he flies uncontrollably back toward the piano. He heads directly toward it like a rocket, heading in both fast and furious. Amiranda gasps, knowing that this cannot lead to a good finish. Unable to slow down, the parrot flaps his wings to brake, and his tail comes in first, as he tries not to crash-land. His attempt is far from successful.

Comically the parrot slides along the top edge of the highly polished piano, hitting the far wall with his brightly feathered noggin; thereby abruptly stopping him dead in his tracks. Upside down he lies there, with his tail-end placed high over his head. Although tousled and ruffled, he is thankful not to have fallen off the edge of the piano like he usually does.

"W-a-r-k!" the parrot exclaims as he tries to shake the consciousness back into his head.

"Are you alright Reynolds?" Amiranda asks, worried about her fine-feathered friend. “Here, I’ll help you,” she tells him.

The princess places Peatie back down atop the piano and hurries over to help the stunned bird. Gently, she strokes the feathers on the parrot’s head so that they perk up again. Reynolds props himself up to stand upright, again losing his balance on the slippery and overly polished piano. He attempts to take flight but it is too late; the piano’s mirrorlike finish is far too slippery for him to maintain his footing. Time and time again, he loses his balance.

Reynolds falls once more, this time sliding forward along the piano, ultimately stopping by heading face first into Peatie. The tame parrot has always been an ace at flying, but not quite as skilled with graceful or even successful landings, being a domesticated animal all his life. Courteously, the kind puppy tries to help the parrot. He nudges the bird upward with his nose. Reynolds returns the favor by taking a quick peck at him; he does not want his help. The parrot flies back to his cage, clearly jealous of the pup.

Reynolds squawks in reply, “No help! Arrk, alright. Wark, alright.”

Chapter 2

French Breakfast

There is a loud thumping noise heard outside the room as the castle's fortress-like wooden door abruptly opens. With a great bang and a loud noise, the door slams against the back wall of the room as it swings open, far unlike the more formal and dignified manner in which it was opened earlier by the butler. The mood in the room immediately changes as the aroma of food permeates throughout. Both Peatie's and Reynolds' eyes light up. They know that it is time to eat.

Just as the pup's mouth starts to water, Amiranda's personal chef,

Kistoffe, pronounced "Keestoff," comes waltzing in. He is always overly-joyous and frolicking about. Today is no different than any other day, as he is always full of love and full of energy. To him, cooking is not only a job, it is a passion of life.

Unlike Jove, who is tall and slender in stature, the chef is a rather short, pudgy man with a roly-poly face. His eyes are overly large and extremely round—shaped like two giant oatmeal cookies. He has large, black pupils that look like two oval-shaped olives. They dance around whenever he laughs, which is quite often. His nose is shaped like a plum tomato and is almost the same rosy-red color. He wears an all-white baker's outfit, complete with a tall, pastry-style hat which is neatly ruffled along its pleats. With him he carries his own handy and generously-oversized wooden pepper mill to grind his own favorite seasoning—strong, fresh, and sneeze-inducing black pepper.

"It is time, it's time! Hee hee," the chef announces, chuckling merrily. "It is zee time for zee breakfast!" he declares with such great enthusiasm.

The chef bounces into the room with a thunderous roar, joyous to serve his highly distinguished guests. Unlike Amiranda, Kistoffe cannot wait to face the day. With such vigor and robust energy, he is always ready to take on the world, although a common, loyal servant he may be.

"Huh huh!" he chuckles again. "It's time, it's time, it's time!" The chef repeats himself, each time getting a little bit louder and growing a little more anxious.

Peatie wags his tail frantically, all too ready to eat. As a small pup that is quickly growing, he is famished and needs his nourishment. Reynolds, fidgety and more impatient than his usual self, flaps his wings in great haste for a delicious meal.

Whenever Kistoffe speaks, the cheerful baker uses an almost

irreverently phony French accent. He utilizes bits and pieces of broken English and French, combining the two languages to form his own unique language. It is unclear whether or not he himself is in fact French or just excessively fond of the culture. Whenever possible, he will translate his own words for Amiranda to understand, although she is already used to both his accent and his language, and usually does not need the help.

Kistoffe goes behind the bar-like kitchen alcove, oddly enough sprinkling pepper all around the room. He starts to fidget with all the utensils, creating a racket, and a mess.

"Good morning, Kistoffe," Amiranda replies politely, "how are you today?"

The princess' tone is somber, still partly immersed in her own thoughts and wishes. She takes a seat at the counter and places Peatie on the stool next to her. The young pup shakes himself the way any normal puppy would, headfirst, then slowly down to his tail. She gently places her hand on the pup, rubbing his ears and neck softly, petting him so he will relax and settle down.

The French chef moves around the kitchen with ease, grabbing exactly what he needs. Clearly, he would be able to do so blindfolded. With his colorful and exaggerated motions, he performs his menial and everyday tasks, such as cooking, with great showmanship. He is almost like a magician in the way he uses his hands to coordinate his motions and overembellish his movement. Preparing the food and presenting it delectably is, undoubtably, his greatest performance.

However ambidextrous the chef might be, by no means does that make him tidy or neat. In fact, to say the least, at times he can be somewhat of a klutz when it comes to making a mess of his work. Although never dropping a plate, the aura that surrounds him is one of a quite carefree nature, yet it is not to be confused with not caring for those around him—especially for his favorite noble princess, Amiranda.

"Huh huh! Je suis magnifique! I am magnificent!" Kistoffe replies kindly, with his great big belly jiggling as he laughs.

"What a be-a-u-ti-ful day!" he continues, exuberantly throwing his hands up in the air, ever-thankful to the wonderful world around him. "What a glorious time to be zee Franch, and to be in l'amour—that is to be in zee love, and to be here in zee spring with zee birds, and zee bees, and zee leaves. Oui, oui! Yes, yes! C'est simply magnifique! It is truly magnificent!"

Reynolds interjects hungrily, "Warrk! Oui oui! Oui oui!" The parrot eagerly mimics the chef's words, utilizing the same thick and overly-emphasized French accent. He lifts up one of the forks with his beak, waiting anxiously to eat.

Kistoffe turns to the young princess, seeing that she is not her usual, and happy self. Curious and concerned, the chef begins to wonder and contemplate. Nevertheless, he always acts jovial, as that is his normal self.

"Et vous, Amiranda? How are you?" The chef pries as he throws a dash of pepper over his shoulder. Perhaps it is a part of some strange, ritualistic gesture.

Amiranda has a deep admiration and affection for the chef, yet at times she does not understand why he is so overly cheerful. Simply put, the chef loves his work and looks forward to preparing meals for anyone who will have a taste of any one of his many specialties. That is, of course, as long as it is French—or how he says "Franch."

"I'm okay, Kistoffe," Amiranda plainly states in reply, although she is not too convincing, neither to the chef nor herself for that matter.

"What are we having for breakfast today?" The princess asks partly out of habit and partly to try to change the subject; she already knows the list of choices which will soon follow in response.

"Huh huh huh," Kistoffe chuckles repeatedly. His great big belly bounces along wholeheartedly with him as he tries to hold his tummy in place. "What would you like? Zee Franch toast, zee Franch omelet, zee Franch bread?" The chef promptly displays the fresh, mouthwatering bread on a tray in a gracefully smooth, sweeping gesture.

"Qu'est-ce que tu aimes? What would you like? Anything with zee pepper of course, of course! Hee hee!" Kistoffe laughs as he sprays more pepper all around. After breathing some in, he lets out a huge sneeze—a sneeze that almost blows the feathers right off of Reynolds.

"Kistoffe, do you always have to make such a mess?" Amiranda asks curiously, as a slight giggle starts in her voice and the dainty ripples of her nose begin to dance, a common display of affection when the princess is timidly amused. "Why must you always spray pepper around—it's not a French custom," she points out, careful not to criticize. Amiranda wiggles her nose in order to defend against the urge to let out a huge sneeze.

"Huh huh! Oui oui!" Kistoffe laughs loudly. "C'est vrai, c'est vrai! It's true, it's true! How I do love zee pepper! It is my favorite of all the spices!"

Kindly, he is not offended by Amiranda's inquisitiveness, but is only more than happy to explain to her his use, or rather abuse, of the spice he so lovingly adores.

"This is true, it is not zee Franch custom, but my mère—that is my Ma-má, she always said it would bring her good luck. So, I always have to spray it everywhere, to bring me good luck! On zee floor, in my food, even in zee bathtub!" Kistoffe answers her question good-humoredly, chuckling heavily in reply. Comically, he sprinkles even more pepper around the room.

"Huh huh! It makes me happy, see?" Kistoffe kindly offers the peppershaker to Amiranda. "Would you care for some Amiranda? It could make you happy too, oui?"

"Just please don't put too much in my breakfast today. Okay Kistoffe?" Amiranda requests politely. "It makes my nose tingle." Once again she unknowingly displays the dainty wrinkles in her nose.

Reynolds sneezes a thunderous sneeze. "Squawk-choo!"

Kistoffe laughs a hearty laugh and everyone is amused—that is, everyone except for Amiranda. Sadly enough, she is numb to the chef's cheerfulness, the amusing comedy of her own pet sneezing uncontrollably, or the fact that there is now pepper all over the kitchen. Her mind is still far off elsewhere.

Although the chef's main duty is to prepare food for the royal princess, he often helps Amiranda by being someone in whom she can confide. This especially goes for things she wants to keep "off the record." She will often share with him her concerns and her own personal thoughts and feelings, as her own family is way too busy to be there for her. The king and queen have countless noble affairs and royal schedules to keep. Never do they have any time left aside to devote or listen to young Amiranda.

Once sidetracked, Kistoffe does not let go of his original question. He is not unlike Amiranda, who is relentless when it comes to someone avoiding her own questions.

"So, my little princess, have you made up your mind? What would you like for zee breakfast?" The French chef places a large dish in front of Amiranda and a big red bowl on the counter for Peatie. Peatie's bowl is nearly twice the size of him and the big, bold letters on the side of it almost dwarf the small pup.

"I dunno, Kistoffe." Amiranda contemplates the question, seeking a neutral answer for something other than the same old "French this" or "French that." She wants to be sure not to offend her eccentric friend. She hesitates, careful to choose the right words.

"I kind of want something different for a change," the princess continues, declaring her passion for something more bold, new, and exciting. As she is caught up in the moment contemplating what life would be like if things were only different, she realizes that she might have possibly offended the chef. She quickly correct herself, complimenting him.

"Not to say that your cooking isn't the best in the world," she continues, trying to backtrack her steps. "Why, 'C'est magnifique!'"

Amiranda tries to annunciate one of Kistoffe's favorite sayings just like the chef, although she is halfhearted in her attempt. It is a meek effort compared to Kistoffe's highly polished accent. After a moment, Amiranda reconfirms her desire for something different. Her tone is very innocent, however there is a certain degree of indecisiveness to it. In reality, she is not exactly sure what it is that she wants.

"It's just that I'm kind of in the mood for something new today," she proclaims as her words take on a deeper meaning within her heart. She picks up her spoon, holding it up to look at her own reflection. She positions it to catch the image out the window, which is somewhat morphed by the shape of the utensil.

Reynolds, impatient for his meal, quickly inches his way up Kistoffe's sleeve. He uses his beak to pull his own body upward and his talons to securely anchor himself to the coat's material. It is a customary practice for the bird to rest on the chef's shoulder while Kistoffe feeds him—almost as customary as Kistoffe wearing his white baker's outfit and sprinkling dashes of pepper all around. Reynolds has taken a keen liking to the chef, and the chef enjoys the parrot's camaraderie. In fact, Kistoffe is the one person Reynolds not only looks up to, but also has great admiration for. After all, a smart pet would never bite the hand from which it feeds.

Kistoffe thinks to himself for a second, and then finally lets out a soft sigh in reply to the princess' desire for something new to be on the menu. After a moment's deliberation, the French chef whimsically replies, "Hmm. Why, zee change, zee change! Oui oui! Zee change is good! Zee leaves change, zee flowers—they change, zee life changes; everything changes. Huh huh!" he chuckles lavishly. Reynolds echoes the chef's laugh as Kistoffe succeeds in getting flour everywhere, trying to make his infamous and delectable French bread.

"How about zee Franch croissants with zee eggs and zee cheese?" Kistoffe asks, unable to give the young princess what she truly wants. The chef's offer of a cheese omelet in French pastry-type bread is definitely not a change for Amiranda. The same goes for anything else the chef or anyone else can offer her.

Amiranda slowly turns her head only to look back toward the window, viewing the great countryside outside. She cannot seem to get her mind off of it—perhaps spring fever has finally set in. Still, she thinks it is something a bit more, as she is never really allowed to visit the outside world, for her own protection. Not anymore anyway. Greatly disappointed, she quickly realizes that some things will never change.

"I was thinking more along the lines of something simple, like cereal." The young princess states her request with that same mystical air as before, indicating she needs to find something more to this world—more than just a change in breakfast.

With her eyes still fixated on the outside, Amiranda does not notice the confused expression on Kistoffe's face when her words are heard.

The French chef stops abruptly when the princess says the word "cereal," for cereal has no connotation or meaning for the culinary talent of a French artiste such as he. To him, that would be like asking Michelangelo to paint using only one color, or for Mozart to play *Chopsticks* on the piano. To do such a thing would surely be underutilizing his refined talents. No, the French chef does not cook cereal, not for anyone.

Kistoffe is astounded by Amiranda's sudden appetite for something so mundane and simple as cereal. Stunned, he asks, "What? Que'est que c'est? What is this?" he translates. "Le cereal?" he asks with his voice pitched high.

"One cannot cook zee cereal," the chef continues, his left brow rising almost straight in midair. "It is not zee fried, zee broiled, zee baked to zee magnifique delicacy. I am zee Franch chef, therefore, I cook zee Franch foods—isn't that true my little friends?"

Peatie yelps and Reynolds squawks a "True, true" in agreement, both eager for a home-cooked meal. Especially one specifically prepared for them, as Kistoffe's cooking is truly and amazingly delectable. Kistoffe's astonishment turns into great joy whenever he talks about food, namely French food. He twirls his spatula about spreading great joy and flour everywhere.

"Oui oui! Oui oui! Zee Franch! Zee Franch!" Reynolds mimics the chef, squawking loudly. There is no doubt that the parrot has great affection toward his devoted food provider.

Skillfully, Kistoffe decides to take a different approach by asking the two starved critics. "And what would you two like, my little friends," he says to them, "zee omelet, zee toast Franch?" The chef proceeds collected and composed, a true culinary master of his cuisine.

"Zee omelet! Zee omelet!" Reynolds replies, bobbing himself up and down. Peatie wags his short tail frantically in agreement.

"Z'omelet. C'est bien! Very good!" the jovial chef says to the two ravenous pets. Once more Peatie's mouth waters with delight.

Kistoffe again poses his question to Amiranda. "Et vous Amiranda?" he asks. Masterfully he breaks open some eggs and whips them up in a large round copper bowl. At all times the French chef remains diligent at his work, acting unphased by the princess' curious desire for an uncooked meal.

"I think I'll just have the French toast today," Amiranda simply replies, with a taste of disappointment coloring her voice. "I guess some things simply cannot be changed," Amiranda thinks to herself as she picks up her small pup. Affectionately she cradles him in her arms. The chef continues cooking … happily.

As Kistoffe scrambles the eggs, the sound of the wire cooking whisk striking against the metal bowl creates a steady rhythmic beat. Reynolds, getting caught up in the music, bobs his head up and down in cadence. Peatie sways to the music, tilting his head to one side and then the other along with the tempo. As usual, the French chef loves to sing as he cooks. He improvises a cheerful "French" cooking song on the spot, which he creates and sings especially for them ...

I am Franch, I am Franch, I am Franch—oui oui!
I am Franch, I am Franch, I am Franch—oui oui!
I cook zee Franch toast and zee Franch bread,
I am Franch, I am Franch, I am Franch. Oui oui!

How 'bout a helping of bread?
You know I'm here to keep you well fed;
I'll twirl my spatula while I'll make a batch full of all
The things that are French 'cause I am Franch. Oui oui!

What is this I hear about cereal?
You know one cannot cook such material;
You can't be serious—you must be delirious;
I only cook zee Franch 'cause I am Franch—oui oui!

I am Franch, I am Franch, I am Franch—oui oui!
I am Franch, I am Franch, I am Franch—oui oui!
I cook zee Franch toast and zee Franch bread,
'Cause I am Franch, I am Franch, I am Franch! Oui oui!

While he is singing, Kistoffe cooks multiple dishes at the same time, using exact precision, his cleanliness falling to the wayside. Simultaneously he whips up some eggs, sautés slices of French toast, and fries several strips of bacon, all while singing and laughing his entire life's cares away. The chef is so diligent in his work that he pays no mind to a little flour spreading here and a dash of pepper scattering there—to him that simply comes with the territory. However, as with any great chef, they tend to use a bit more seasoning than they ought.

As a grand finale, the chef ends his song spreading his arms outward in the way of a true "extraordinaire," again giving thanks for the glorious world around him. A huge puff of flour spreads all over Peatie and Reynolds, mushrooming straight up into the air as it explodes. Everyone is thrilled by Kistoffe's performance. All are laughing or yelping delightfully, including Princess Amiranda.

"Oh, that was wonderful Kistoffe!" Amiranda exclaims, clapping her hands affectionately in gratitude. She stands up and twirls around, gently holding the sides of her dress out to her side. Peatie shakes off the flour and then watches her closely, following her graceful, flowing movements with every tilt of his head.

Elegantly the princess spins around for a moment, before suddenly slowing down. It is almost like a spinning top that loses its momentum—it turns very fast and then releases all of its energy as it completely winds down. Her thoughts suddenly change to what is really on her mind. She quickly releases the pleats of her gown, making her dress appear lifeless in comparison to before, and her body grows limp once again.

She continues, "but you know what you want to be. What I mean is that you are *who* you want to be."

Amiranda takes a deep breath, herself being clearly caught up in the moment. "Oh, how I wish I knew what life will be like for me when I'm older. Will I fall in love? Will I marry? Who will I marry?" She pauses briefly. "The future is so unclear to me now."

The princess sighs as she sits back down. She places her head atop of her hands, with her elbows on the table. Feeling listless and unsettled, a terrible feeling for anyone to have, she simply has no other choice but to hurry up and wait.

"All I can see is me, still here in this place; I will be surrounded by these same four walls for years and years to come." Again, Amiranda is careful not to pout. "Let's face it, I'll be stuck here for the rest of my life."

The expression on Kistoffe's face is utter astonishment, seeing the princess in a way he has never noticed before. Yet at the same time he is quite empathetic to the princess' need for something more. To him it had always appeared that Amiranda had everything anyone could want right at her fingertips. After all, she is a lady-to-be, with many fortunes of wealth awaiting her and a perfect lifestyle to match. The chef holds up his ladle and shakes it vigorously to try to remind the young princess of all that she has.

"Oh Amiranda, you have such zee beautiful life," he reminds her, looking all around at the lush room they are in and all the riches that surround her. "Why, you have more than anyone could ever imagine. And you are such a pretty girl, soon to be a lady. Someday zee entire kingdom of Luxing will be *yours!*" Although true, his words are little comfort to the princess.

The French chef places a plate filled with French toast along with some scrambled eggs and several strips of bacon on the counter for her. Kistoffe always prepares more food than anyone can actually ever finish.

He then hands Peatie's bowl over to her. Amiranda places the bowl filled with food on the floor by her feet for Peatie, who almost drowns in its size. The young pup keeps pushing the bowl along while trying to eat, ending up a few feet from where he originally started. Reynolds, who is still perched on the chef's shoulder, gets hand-fed the pieces of the omelet he had "ordered."

After a moment's deliberation, Amiranda finally replies to the chef.

Again, she does not let go of her own original thought.

"I know my father wants me to be a 'lady,'" the princess hesitates, once again choosing her words carefully before continuing. "But I don't know if I want to spend my whole life in this kingdom of Luxing. I want to meet people, do things, explore places—be free."

She twirls her fork around in her hand, her mind a half million miles away, fluttering away like a butterfly. "Luxing would do fine without me. Why, I would have the whole world to explore for myself." The sparkling reflection of her overly polished silver fork that she is twirling can be seen reflected in Amiranda's eyes.

Peatie and Reynolds continue eating, each of them strictly focused on their food.

"Oh Amiranda, you have plenty of time to grow up," Kistoffe reminds her while he attempts to tidy up a bit. He pushes some flour into a large pile and leaves it there for the butler to clean up. Perhaps some of his untidiness stems from him not having to clean up after himself. He continues, "Let it come when it's z'ready. Why, you have grown up so much now. I remember as if yesterday you were running in zee fields, just a little girl playing. Why, you were only up to here on me." He points to his big round belly, letting out a slight chuckle, reminiscing about days long past. Sadly he realizes that the young princess is growing up so quickly. She is not so young anymore.

Timidly, Amiranda takes small bites, eating her breakfast in between conversing with the chef. She shuffles the food around on her plate, thinking about some of the things he has said. Kistoffe has always been a dear friend to her. He is much more than just a caretaker and more akin to being a caregiver, and she truly trusts his judgment. Still, she thinks that this time she has to take a stand for herself.

"I'm not allowed in the fields anymore," Amiranda retorts, "that was all before." She hints at some hushed, godforsaken incident that happened there long ago. "Everything is so different now, yet everything is still all the same. At least to me it is, day after day. All I want is a taste of something new." The princess does not realize her own play on words. She takes another small nibble of her breakfast, but she is mostly just moving the small pieces of French toast around on her plate.

For a moment, all is quiet. Kistoffe understands Amiranda's frustration, but at the same time also wishes that he could live life as easily as she does—having everything neatly catered to her. Still, the chef never shows sorrow, and he never gets depressed. No matter what, his constant carefree spirit and his unchanging love for the life around him always shine through. Both Reynolds and Peatie are now done with their meal, which only adds to the temporary silence.

Kistoffe continues to work his civil duties as a chef, all the while thinking of what Amiranda just said. It is not that he does not want to address the princess' concerns, but more that it is not rightfully his place to do so. Typically, it is Amiranda's nanny that gives her the most advice and support in growing up, but for some reason, the nanny has not been around as much as she usually is. Hence, the young princess has been addressing her concerns to the members of the staff more and more, which is certainly understandable. Still, Kistoffe's robust energy and his dedication for cooking never quite fully allow for Amiranda's words to fully sink in.

Suddenly, once again the thick wooden castle door swings open. Jove hurriedly reenters the room carrying a silver tray over one of his shoulders, while holding it steady with one hand. A white linen towel is neatly draped over his other arm. The butler stops dead in his tracks, seeing the clutter they had all created. One would think he would surely be used to it by now.

"Oh my! What a mess Kistoffe!" Jove exclaims, slapping his head firmly with the palm of his hand. "You never cease to amaze me. I am quite sure that I will have the honor of enjoying the better half of my day tidying up after you!" Remnants of flour, pepper, salt, and egg are spread all around the kitchen area.

"I'm very sorry, monsieur," Kistoffe chuckles wholeheartedly, lightening up the situation. "Would you care for some pepper?" he asks the butler, while kindly offering him the peppershaker. Humorously, he sprinkles another light dash. "I will try to keep it down next time," the chef promises. Jove knows that promise all too well, hearing it again and again, practically every day.

"Now, if you will excuse me, I must be off!" Kistoffe announces. "It's time! It's time! I will see you tomorrow Amiranda! Remember what I told you," he reminds her, "there is zee time for everything! Oui oui. C'est vrai! It's true! Huh huh!" The French chef cheers and exits joyously, continuing to sprinkle fresh-ground pepper everywhere as he leaves the room.

Reynolds lets out another huge sneeze. "What a mess, what a mess! Squawk-Choo!"

FLOU

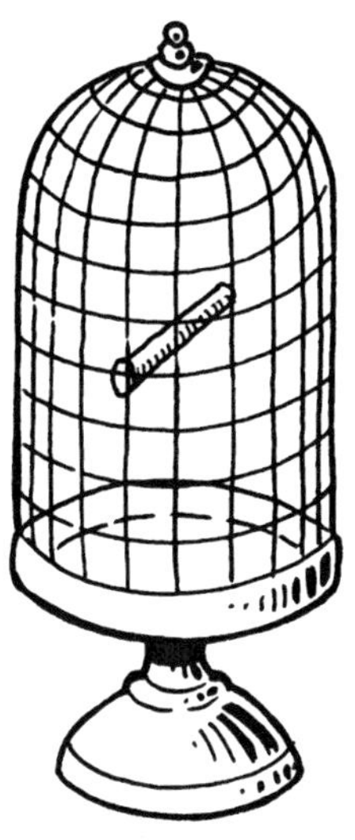

Chapter 3

Caged

The more Jove looks around the room, the more and more of a mess he sees—the mess created and left behind by the chef. Even though he is faced with this challenge continually, the stately butler is always amazed by the monstrosity and mayhem that Kistoffe leaves behind. Nevertheless, the distinguished butler always remains well-mannered, professional, and dignified.

"If only the king knew of what truly goes on around here," Jove proclaims, mostly muttering to himself. "I'm quite sure that he would commend me with a medal, or perhaps even place *me* in charge of the entire kingdom itself. Lord knows I deserve it!" the dignified butler praises himself for a job well done. He tends to pat himself on the back at every chance he can take.

"Did you practice your piano lesson Amiranda?" he asks the princess, already *knowing* the answer. Jove starts to clear off the counter by placing all the bowls, plates, and utensils on his tray. That is, all but Amiranda's, which was hardly touched.

In a daydream somewhere far away, Amiranda suddenly recognizes the mention of her name. Immediately thereafter she realizes Jove's question that was directed at her. "Hmm?" she finally replies, her eyes slowly refocusing on the situation. "Oh, excuse me Jove—I'm terribly sorry, I forgot. I promise I'll do twice as much tomorrow," she graciously apologizes. The princess thinks about the conversation she had with Kistoffe moments earlier before finally letting out a light sigh; her mind starts drifting off once again.

"Amiranda, do not let your father catch wind of this," Jove cautions her. "I am here to ensure that *all* of your royal duties are kept." He pauses for a moment as he regains track of his original thought. "Now where did I put that broom?" he finally asks himself, looking around the room at the great mess. He tries to figure out what he should do first as the room has gone from pure spotless to complete mayhem. Amiranda continues to nibble on her food, prodding the French toast with the prongs of her fork.

As the butler opens the closet door in search of a broom, the entire contents falls directly on top of him—letting out a huge crash and yet another large billowing cloud of white powder. More flour disperses everywhere, covering the butler's black, custom-tailored suit. Peatie, the small young pup that was mostly brown only seconds ago, is now a snowball of pure white.

The parrot quickly exclaims, "The butler did it! The butler did it!"

Trying hard not to laugh, Amiranda covers her mouth with the cup of her hand. She giggles into it politely, attempting not to let the sound out. The princess is all too amused by Jove's bumbling display of comedy, uncommon as it may be. It is not often that the distinguished butler becomes all disheveled and unkempt, as he appears now.

"Oh be quiet, you overgrown feather duster," Jove squawks back at the bird lightheartedly, but obviously flustered by the clutter. "I told your father we should have had that bird stuffed when we found him," he tells Amiranda teasingly. Although there is sarcasm in his remark, he is truly rather fond of the parrot, and only being witty to help alleviate his frustration.

"Now just look at this mess. I do not see why you can't use your parents' chef instead—he is far more organized and much tidier," Jove professes, as he begins to dust himself off. "Why must everyone in this family have their own personal chef?" he questions. The butler then continues to clean up the counter using a small silver-handled brush and dustpan, careful not to further untidy himself or his tailor-made suit.

Amiranda picks up Peatie from the floor and places him gently onto her lap. The flour-covered puppy shakes the white powder off of him, creating another large, billowing plume of dust. Caught in the midst of it, Amiranda gets a small dot of flour on the tip of her nose. Her faithful companion courteously licks her nose clean, tickling it in the process. She lets out another slight giggle. Then, still not paying complete attention to Jove, Amiranda continues to drift further and further away.

"Jove, what's the outside world like?" Amiranda asks, letting her own inquisitiveness once again get the better of her. The immediate world around her, however, is the furthest thing from her mind.

"I mean not just the town of Luxing, but what's past this kingdom, past the forest?" Amiranda stands up, taking one step closer to the window. "Is there a grand and marvelous place somewhere out there; a place with adventures and happenings beyond our wildest imagination?" Although strange, her question is raised with all practical seriousness.

The butler interrupts her thoughts.

"Well it is certainly no place for a young girl like yourself," he warns her using a strict, cautious tone of voice. Jove looks at her, watching her carefully, while successfully cleaning the counter at the same time; he wipes it down with a dampened towel.

"Especially concerning the *Deciduous Forest*," he continues telling her, now paying more attention to the duties to which he must attend. The counters shine as they did before, the butler utilizing the condensation of his own breath to revive them back to their full brilliance.

"Why Amiranda, you shouldn't even be thinking about such a thing," Jove states as he wipes up the last bit of crumbs from the floor. "You still have so much to learn and so much to experience before your father ever lets you into the outside world—let alone any forest." He looks at her once again; the princess is still looking out onto the countryside. "That is, if he ever lets you outside."

It is said that every statement holds some truth, however, this statement could not be any truer. Amiranda's family has always been overly protective of their only daughter, and with good reason, but no one is really sure what that reason is. The simple truth of the matter is that most people have forgotten exactly why things are they way they are. For her, it has become just a fact of life, just like the sun rising at dawn or the blossoming of flowers that come with each rising spring. It is a fact that the princess must come to terms with, no matter how hard she tries to do otherwise.

Satisfied with his accomplishment, Jove places his towel on the tray, next to the rest of the soiled dishes. He leaves Amiranda's dish on the counter, as most of her food still remains uneaten.

"You are a lady in waiting as far as royalty is concerned; the outside world is no place for a young lady like yourself," Jove adds, stating the sheer reality of the situation.

Amiranda turns around and for once looks directly at Jove. "I'll never get any experience of the outside world if I'm never *in* the outside world," she retorts, almost losing her innocent composure for the first time in her life. The princess quickly realizes her words are nothing but stale air. Surrendering for a moment, she places her remaining French toast in Peatie's bowl, her own appetite left unfulfilled.

"I'm seventeen now and I'm ready to accept new challenges and explore new things for myself," she argues reasonably, as if she were talking to her own father and not the hired help. "I want to experience things for myself—rather than having everyone else telling me what to do, how to feel, what to think, and how to behave." Amiranda pauses, perhaps seeking feedback, perhaps seeking the full effect of her words to sink in.

"What do you think, Jove?" she asks in a high-pitched tone. The princess places her now empty plate on Jove's silver platter. She does not realize that by asking Jove for his opinion, she clearly contradicts the very thing she wishes most for—her independence.

"I am merely a butler; I do not get paid to think," the butler refutes, stating the obvious truth in the matter. Trying to stay professional and remain uninvolved in the affairs of the household, he continues, "Your father entrusts me with your welfare and that is precisely what I see to." Jove is firm, yet fair to Amiranda, choosing the words he uses quite carefully. Again, being a professional, he states only what needs to be said.

As Jove finishes cleaning up, there is a moment of silence felt as his words gradually sink in—both to Amiranda and also to himself. He too is realizing that there really is no one for the princess to privately confide in, especially regarding her own personal family matters. Amiranda is growing up fast, and her everyday problems are growing more and more complex every day.

"Off the record," Jove continues, speaking to her this time as a friend, "there is a time and place for everything. When that time comes, you will know." He picks up his tray and then exits through the door, having fulfilled his obligatory duties there, and having more duties to perform elsewhere in the castle.

Still preoccupied, Amiranda tries to thank Jove for his sound words of advice. Her gratitude is too late. "Thank you, Jo—." Her words are cut off midsentence as the door shuts behind him. Unlike Kistoffe who exits in a thunderous, joyous roar; the only sound heard when Jove exits is the subtle click of the latch as the door closes shut.

"But how will I know?" she ponders to herself. All alone now, with the exception of her two pets, her question is directed at the door, as Jove is totally unable to hear her. Quietly, Amiranda picks up her pup, cradling him in her arms.

"Okay Reynolds," she tells her pet parrot, "you know the rules. I have to go upstairs for a while so into the cage you go. I'll check up on you later—I promise." Amiranda nods one side of her head toward the cage, politely gesturing for the parrot to fly in while she is still cradling Peatie.

"In the cage, in the cage," Reynolds squawks mockingly, hearing those same words spoken to him all the time. Reluctantly, Reynolds waddles his way along the counter before leaping off of it and hopping into his cell. He is clearly used to having full reign of the household, or at least these quarters.

Amiranda latches the cage door, shutting him in. "Now I don't want to find this cage unlocked when I come back down here either. I'll let you fly around some more later."

The princess carries her small pup to the grand marble staircase. She gently places Peatie down at the bottom of the stairs and picks up her shoes, which lay there resting on the floor. One by one, she puts them on, holding onto the railing for support as she carefully leans over. Unhurriedly, she then makes her way up the staircase. Peatie clumsily follows Amiranda, shimmying his way up every few steps.

Chapter 4

Amiranda's Room

Unlike the rest of the estate, Amiranda's bedroom is quite modest and practical. It is like most ordinary girls' rooms are, with frills of lace and girlie-type trinkets placed all around. The room is simple yet elegant; everything is kept very neat, clean, and tidily organized. The princess places extreme emphasis on having everything placed in its precise location within her room. There are many special points of interest carefully distributed throughout the princess' quarters, all of which are just waiting to be discovered. Yet, there is never really anyone to discover them.

The princess' bedroom set is reasonably sized, consisting of only four main pieces: a mirrored vanity, a nightstand, a tall dresser, and a four-post canopy bed. The furnishings are all creamy-white in color. The edges and handles are lavishly decorated in solid twenty-four karat gold. Several small hand-painted flowers adorn each one of the vanity's and dresser's drawers; her bedroom set is very cute and childlike in appearance, just like the princess herself.

Amiranda enters the room with Peatie walking right beside her every inch of the way. She is now fully dressed wearing a long, flowing white gown that any normal princess would be fond of. Nevertheless, she is somber and solemn in her mood, far unlike her normal and usual self. She would much rather be outside playing in her casual wear than indoors, all dressed up, and all alone.

The princess takes a few moments to look around the room, as if taking inventory of all her belongings. She is intrigued by everything and very tactile when it comes to observing all that is around. Even though she knows every inch of her room by heart, it is as though she is looking at everything for the very first time, lost in her own small world.

Amiranda walks over to her night stand, on top which rests a rather large fish tank. Within the rectangular-shaped tank, one single, solitary, and undersized fish swims around by her lonesome. Her pet goldfish would resemble any other typical pet goldfish, except for the fact that she is black and has two oversized eyes protruding from either side of her head. Her small body, outsized by her large, flowing fins, wiggles along whenever she swims. The tank, like the rest of the castle, is greatly oversized for a fish so small.

Adjacent to the tank, strategically placed just to the right of it, there is an elegant jewelry box made from richly polished dark cherrywood. The display case's two front glass panel doors show off the young princess' modest and practical jewelry. The mirrored back wall of the showcase enhances the jewelry's sparkling radiance, as it shimmers luminously within the walls of the case.

Neatly hung in a row, there are several small gold-colored bracelets, some stylish charms, other trinkets, and one centrally positioned necklace with a heart-shaped locket dangling daintily from it. None of Amiranda's jewelry is overly extravagant or flashy, but all are delicate and dainty. Again, special care is taken to place emphasis that less is more, mirroring the young princess' taste.

Just to the right of the tank, symmetrically balancing the jewelry box on the opposite side of it is a beautiful porcelain figurine of a small girl. The pale-faced, blue-eyed doll is put proudly out on display. The delightfully exuberant figurine is wearing a lace bonnet on top of her head, and part of her blonde, curly hair can be seen peeking out from under it. Holding a red bouquet of flowers between her partially muffed hands, she is sophisticatedly dressed in white satin. She also sports a red velvet coat which matches her colorful rose bouquet exquisitely. The doll has a small, red ribbon neatly positioned in the center of her blouse, just like the small lace ribbons sewn onto all of Amiranda's nightgowns and dresses.

Directly above the princess' night table, a number of small portraits line her bedroom wall. The neatly hung images contain various painted portraits of the young princess growing up and her royal family—neither of which are ever in the same picture. All of the pictures are either of Amiranda or her family, but sadly never of Amiranda *with* her family. Still, she holds these pictures and memories dear to her heart.

Amiranda's white lace canopy bed is positioned against one wall of the room, with its headboard standing just adjacent to the room's entryway. The bed is neatly trimmed with a pearl-white ruffled bed skirt and a lavender-colored bedspread that has images of pink flowers printed on it. Meticulously, the entire ensemble matches the room's soft, mauve-colored walls.

The door frame is also neatly trimmed as there are individually hand-painted stencils of pink flowers that bud off of emerald-green vines, making the room appear vibrant and alive. The likeness very much resembles the lovely pink roses that are growing and climbing directly outside her bedroom window. The flowers rise delicately to the ceiling, with their vines wavering along in a serpentine-like pattern, giving the room a very natural and outdoorsy feel.

Surprisingly for a castle as large as this, Amiranda's room is quite small. It has only one window, which exists in the center of the far wall of the room. Compared to the rest of the room's size, the window is of great proportion; it consumes most of the bedroom wall.

As interesting as her bedroom truly is, the princess is not fully satisfied or even partially intrigued by all that lies within it. Once again, she reverts to looking out the window, turning to the outside world, seeking some sort of comfort. Overlooking the westerly horizon, Amiranda kneels at the great window, gazing out to the vast countryside—the same vast countryside over which she will someday reign.

Amiranda can often be seen here, with a bird's eye view from being so high up, silently watching everything. In the morning she would carefully study the daylight dawning as it begins to light up the countryside, smiling upon it kindly as if to greet the day a warm hello. In the evening she would stare at the setting sun as it reverently vanishes behind the forest trees, kissing the horizon softly as if to wish the day a fond good night. No matter what time it was, she would always look at the pond in the near distance below, only a mere stone's throw away from her window. The grassy field lay just beyond, but still within earshot, and the mysterious dark forest was about a longbow arrow's reach away.

Currently, it is midday and the sun radiantly pours in. It illuminates through the great window and shines directly down upon the princess and her pup, creating a warm glow on their faces. Like a statue, Amiranda stares into the world outside, her gaze permeating through the thick windowpane. Both her mind and her heart remain still, filled with her own inner silence.

In the far distance, just to the left of the forest and high on a hill, small parts of the town of Luxing can now be seen. The princess can take in only what she sees of the kingdom—the very tippy tops of the small buildings, the town of Luxing's one and only church with its steeple raised way up high in the sky, and the children at the school all out at play, who all look like small ants traveling in the distance. She would love to someday see the town for herself and play and interact with the children, but unfortunately she knows that she will never be given the chance. As always, she is abiding by her father's strict wishes.

Unable to see the town too well, Amiranda focuses her attention on the nearby pond. She silently watches the pond which is teeming with life—vibrant, colorful, beautiful, wonderful life. It is a life that Amiranda only wishes she had. Most of the pond's lively activity goes on unnoted by the princess, as she is too caught up in her own stillness to notice any of it today. She sits there, motionless, taking it all in. The silence is briefly broken by the young princess' own yearning for something more …

"There's got to be so much out there," Amiranda reassures herself, wishing hopefully. Quietly, she stares off into the distance, far beyond the forest's trees, toward the faint outlines of the mountainsides that reach up and touch the sky. "Surely there must be more to life than just this," she continues, referring to her life set before her with its many present-day boundaries. "There are worlds to explore, mysterious places to visit, enchanting mysteries to ponder, and intriguing people to meet."

Compared to the vast array of land before her and the great window around her, the young princess appears exaggeratedly small in the window frame. If viewed from a distance, her silhouette would almost appear to be just a small dot compared to the rest of her surroundings. For another moment, she watches on silently; nothing out of the ordinary happens.

Unable to notice anything of interest occurring outside and fearing sheer boredom, the disenchanted princess sighs, taking in a large, deep breath of air. Pushing firmly against the windowsill, she then props herself up off the floor, yawns, and stretches. Amiranda walks over to her fish tank and kneels down before it resting on one knee. Peatie follows her every step of the way, then takes rest at the soles of her feet.

Intensely she gazes into her fish tank, with her own image partially reflecting in the glass, she examines the fish's rather dark and lonely world. The aquarium is sparsely decorated, ornamented only with a small replica of a stone castle, which has a stone bridge for the fish to swim or hide under. The bottom of the tank is lined with a deep blue-colored gravel, which identically matches the mysterious mystic-blue color of Amiranda's eyes.

Her pet fish, or "Molly" as she affectionately calls her, swims around the tank slowly in circles—entrapped by the aquarium's thick glass walls.

Amiranda has loved and cared for her for many years, and never noticed her acting unhappily—that is, perhaps until now. It is unclear if Molly is sick, sad, or if it is just an animal instinct reflecting Amiranda's own emotions. Softly, the princess talks to herself, almost as if she was seeking advice from her small aquatic friend.

"The future is undetermined; isn't it?" Amiranda asks, nearly doubting herself. "Destiny must happen to everyone sooner or later," she hesitates for a moment; "when will it be my turn?"

Still on one knee, Amiranda picks up her puppy Peatie, who always remains ever so loyal and faithful, and always at her side. She places one hand under his belly and the other hand on his backside to support his bottom. The reflection of the two inseparable friends can be seen in the crystal-clear glass of the tank, morphed only by the watery refraction and the many bubbles that sporadically arise from within.

"I'll always be stuck here, in this castle, trying to pretend to be something I'm not." Again, the young princess is careful not to pout, as that would not only be undignified, but more importantly, of no use. "I just want to be a normal girl," she explains wishfully. "I'm just not cut out to be a princess." Amiranda places Peatie down beside her and returns to her window, gazing out once more.

"If only my father could see things my way; I'm sure he would understand." Amiranda speaks to herself out loud, wishing only that her father could hear her words. "I'm sure he would want me to be happy." She pauses, again thinking of all the possibilities. "If only things were different," she whispers. Fixed in thought, Amiranda starts to sing to herself …

What would life be like
To feel life's full meaning?
What would I give to
Live the life I'm dreaming?
In a world where a princess
Lives for a higher ground;
Oh, I'll always hear the sound
Of what my heart feels,
What my heart sees.

If only they could understand
That I'd embrace this world
And take it by the hand.
I'd learn everything that I can be
If only I can be, what I can be.

Amiranda's Room

What would life be like to live like
What my heart sees?
What would life be like
To feel life's full meaning?
What would I give to
Live this life I'm dreaming?
What my heart sees.

"Amiranda, are you alright?" An elderly woman's concerned but sweet voice faintly interrupts from downstairs. "What's going on up there?" the woman's voice calls, her footsteps drawing nearer.

Amiranda is quickly alerted by the call. She softly yet hastily cautions both Peatie and Molly on the arrival of their guest, they all know the drill.

"Hurry, Nana's coming up the stairs," she whispers anxiously. "She must not find out that we're not studying," she tells them.

Peatie knocks over a book onto Amiranda's pillow, which opens up exactly as planned—right to the middle. Amiranda projects her voice louder in reply, "I'm fine, Nana." With quick thinking, the young princess improvises an excuse to hopefully cover all of the commotion made. "I'm just rehearsing a play," she explains, calling back out loud.

Amiranda lights her night candle to make it appear as though she is reading. Peatie curls up on the bed, resting his head by the book as if to read along. Nana's footsteps echo louder as she approaches the door; closer and closer she is getting to Amiranda's room.

With a great big belly flop, the princess jumps onto her bed. Acting nonchalantly, she kicks her legs up in the air behind her, swinging them back and forth. She wants it to appear as though nothing out of the ordinary is going on. A respectful soft, short knock is heard at the door.

"Come in," says Amiranda calmly, casually thumbing through the pages of her book. The bedroom door gently swings open; the princess' nanny stands before her in the doorway.

Amiranda's Nana is a medium to slightly heavyset woman, with a big ball of salt and pepper-colored hair. Her beehive-type hairdo is placed upright, making the short elderly woman appear much taller than she actually is, and she has a loose bun of hair. A matching yellow ribbon holds her hair neatly in place, tied in a pretzel-like bow in the back of her head. She is wearing a light-pink house robe, which color closely matches Amiranda's bedspread, and a canary-yellow apron that is trimmed with lace around her neck and the edges of her sleeves.

Even though the elderly woman is somewhat advanced in years, Amiranda's nanny is still very youthful-looking and about as sharp as a tack. Given her years, she is considered to be a seasoned veteran in terms of her knowledge and wisdom. Nevertheless, Nana still possesses a youthful complexion and radiant countenance about her, atypical of women even half her age. The princess' nanny looks around the room, already knowing that the princess had not been studying.

"Amiranda, are you daydreaming again?" she questions, all too knowingly. "You better quit your wild-eyed imaginative schemes and focus some of that energy on your schoolwork," Nana warns her in her own sweet, yet effective, way.

Although they are of no real ancestral relation, Amiranda and her nanny have built a special relationship like the usual bond between a typical grandmother and her own special grandchild. Unlike a typical grandmother and grandchild however, Amiranda's nanny is far more

like a mother to Amiranda—a mother that she never truly had. More importantly, she is Amiranda's best friend. That is, of course, besides her faithful pup, Peatie. Nana has brought up the princess ever since she was a tiny baby, and the two of them now share a strong love for one another. Often, one knows what the other is thinking before anything is ever said. The same holds true today.

"Nana, you know I don't go to school," Amiranda retorts, both matter-of-factly and kindly. She closes her book, and the slight wind created by the pages coming together forces the lighted candle to extinguish.

"You know what I mean," the sweet elderly woman courteously corrects her. Amiranda sits herself upright on the bed, allowing her Nana to sit beside her, which she does. "It is my responsibility to make sure you keep up with your royal studies and your father's schedule."

“My father’s schedule, my father’s schedule—” Amiranda hastily interrupts, repeating her Nana’s words and forgetting her own manners for just a second. She turns her head, distracted by the world outside.

“All anyone ever cares about is my father’s schedule. What about *my* schedule?” Amiranda quickly realizes her frustration stems from her own immediate family, and not from her Nana, so there is no use pouting. After all, reality is reality, and Amiranda has learned that she just has to deal with it.

The princess takes a deep breath, calming herself for the moment. Fiddling with the lace frills of her dress, she looks down, attempting to preoccupy her mind with some other kind thoughts. She vacantly stares at her dress, her shoes, and finally the floor below her feet. Still, only one thought reoccurs. Softly, Amiranda remarks to herself, “Why, I never even had a chance to be a kid.…”

It is a fact that is all too well known to both of them. The princess never did have a chance to be a normal kid and do what normal kids do. She never got to go to school with the other children, play in the fields with the other children, or even be invited to social events with other children. No birthday parties, no sleepovers, no outdoor activities or games—nothing. She has always been too busy trying to live the life of a princess.

“Amiranda,” Nana replies with a strict, yet sweet, tone of authority.

“Y—es,” Amiranda replies, putting some length into her response.

“You know I love you,” she tells her. This time, the princess’ nanny speaks to her in a softer and gentler manner, but with a greater amount of conviction in her voice. Nana looks deep into Amiranda’s eyes, stressing the genuineness of her sincerity and truthfulness in her tone. Amiranda looks back into her nanny’s eyes, making eye contact for the moment.

"Y—e—s." Amiranda lengthens her reply even more, realizing her Nana's point before it is even stated. She knows her Nana almost as well as her Nana knows her. The sweet elderly woman softly grasps hold of one of the princess' hands as she gently begins to coax her hair, stroking it gently with the palm of her hand. Amiranda tilts her head down, staring back down into her own lap. She knows exactly what her nanny is about to say.

"And you love your Nana too, right?"

Peatie looks up at Nana, wagging his tail, confirming his affection for the sweet nanny. There is a brief moment of silence as she waits for a response.

"Of course I do, I didn't mean it that way but—" Amiranda cuts herself off in midsentence. She doesn't know exactly what to say or how to say it. Once more, the princess looks straight into her Nana's eyes. The two have many caring so-called "mother-daughter" talks, but somehow, this one is different.

"I know you didn't, Amiranda." Nana tells her, patting the princess' knee with one hand in order to help console her. "I've known you for many years now, nearly all of your life, in fact," she continues, trying to find the right words to say. "And unlike your father, I've *known* you." Nana makes her points emphatically, but also with a deep sincerity. It is clearly not meant as an insult to her father or to even toot her own horn, nor is it ever taken that way, given the basic facts of the situation.

Nana pauses for a second. She is either trying to think about what she is going to say or trying to let her point sink in. Perhaps it is a little bit of both. Whichever one it may be, Amiranda clearly gets the picture.

"Who talked your father into getting little Peatie?" she continues, asking the question skillfully. With Nana, the words she chooses are like moves in a chess game, strategically positioning the pieces to achieve a positive result. Peatie wags his tail vigilantly, letting out a sharp, high-pitched yelp in agreement.

"You did." Amiranda is humbled by her Nana's precise line of questioning.

"And who was it that sewed the most gorgeous gown for you to wear on your birthday, and made you that magnificent cake as I remember?" Nana is partially gloating now, smiling, to help lighten the mood.

"I know your point, Nana," the young princess reassures her Nana in agreement. However, somewhere in the back of her own mind, she wishes that her own parents were the ones to do all of those great things for her—even if it were only sometimes.

Amiranda continues, "I do love you *very much*, but it's just that I have had parents all this time. Where were they when I was growing up?"

Amiranda emphatically displays both her love and her sincerity for her Nana. At the same time, in the way that she expresses herself, there is a particular sense of disappointment about her parent's lack of love, support, and even presence in her life. If only she were a normal girl, with a normal family.

"Amiranda, you know I can only be responsible for my own doings or misdoings." Nana pauses once again for a brief second, trying to think of how to best convey her point. "However, I do know your father cares for you very much. I can see it in the way that he looks out for you. He is concerned for you and your well-being. And as for your mother ..."

Nana pauses again, for the same reason. "I know deep down inside that she regrets not having a relationship with you like the one you and I share." She picks up Amiranda's hands, holding onto them tightly. "Maybe one day you both will have that relationship," she tells her, changing her tone to one softer and a bit more sorrowful. "One day when I'm away," the elderly woman whispers to herself, beneath her own breath.

Overhearing the remark, perhaps accidentally or perhaps unintentionally, her words take a moment to sink in. Amiranda has never known life without having her beloved Nana by her side. After all, she is really the only one to whom Amiranda can tell her deepest secrets and share her own feelings with. At least, she is the only one who will care enough to listen and to do something about it. Clearly, the princess is startled by the implications of such a statement.

"You're not going anywhere, are you?" Amiranda worriedly asks. Peatie's eyes become watery, looking half-fearful, half-sad. "I love you too much for you to go away, you're the only one I have," she reminds her.

"Now Amiranda," Nana interjects, trying to maintain control of the situation as well as lighten it. "There comes a time in life when everyone must move on."

With those words said, she stands up, gently brushing her gown with her hands to smooth out any wrinkles formed from sitting upon Amiranda's bed. It also helps her to avoid making eye contact with her closest friend and most loved one, the young princess. She continues, "I'm afraid your nanny's getting old and I won't always be around to look after you."

This time, Nana is the one who is staring out the window. For once it is she who does not know the right words to say.

Amiranda follows her nanny's motion, rising up from the bed. "You're not sick, are you Nana?" she jumps up questioning, not really wanting to know the answer, if it is true.

Nana turns around only to avoid the question altogether. "Now never mind," she tells her, regaining their eye contact. "As I remember correctly, you have some studying to do." The nanny's words are a feeble, yet effective, attempt to change the topic of conversation. She lets out a slight cough, but tries to mask any hints of ailment. Nana remains standing as she seats Amiranda back down onto the bed, opening the book for her.

Without another word being spoken, Amiranda silently knows the answer to her own question.

"Is there anything I can do?" Amiranda asks in a fairly undisguisable, worried manner. She doesn't know how to react; she looks up at Nana while thumbing inattentively at the pages of her book. Many thoughts race through the princess' mind, which as a result, overload her senses.

"Now you never mind me," Nana reassures her, trying again to change the topic. "Dinner will be soon—so you better hit those books," she tells her as she walks over to the door. "Oh, and as for next time, try to have Peatie pick you out something other than a cookbook." Nana looks back one last time before she gently closes the door behind her.

"Yes, Nana," Amiranda agrees, although the door is already shut. The princess realizes that she is starting to make a habit of talking to closed doors. She pauses for a second, contemplating.

"Peatie," she calls over to her faithful companion. Peatie's eyes widen. "Something's terribly wrong with Nanny," she tells him nervously. "We have just got to find out what it is. Why, there must be some way we can help her."

Amiranda looks out past the pond, to the open green grass meadow, then up toward the bright midday sky, and finally all across the horizon, to the vast, beautiful world outside. The mysterious dark forest looms in the distance.

"We just have to find out what it is," she whispers decisively. Peatie yelps in agreement.

Chapter 5

The Magistrate

The magistrate's room is extremely elegant yet simple, much like the rest of the estate, but far more impressive. An area filled with class and distinction, this is where all the royal business meetings and grand social balls take place. The room is, simply put, enormous, in every sense of the word.

Magnificently hung nearly twenty-five feet in the air, three giant chandeliers cascade down from the ceiling; they elegantly light the space. Not all of the same size, the two slightly smaller chandeliers on the outside offset and balance the much larger and far grander one in the center. The shimmering display of light created by the fixture's many large crystals sparkles off the highly polished wood floor of the king's ballroom.

Despite the three incredibly large chandeliers that illuminate the room, the ballroom is rather dark; it is void of any direct or outside sunlight. Heavy velvet curtains restrict the day's light from entering the space. They cover the ballroom's main windows, which are purposefully hidden. The room's opulent draperies are colored in a brilliant jade-emerald green; they are a few shades darker than the room's sea-green walls.

Around the perimeter of the ballroom, neatly hung along each wall, there are numerous oil paintings depicting distinct royal family members, all of which are put proudly out on display. Each portrait is separated by a candlelit sconce. The many portraits tell that the princess' family has reigned over the town of Luxing for many years, as there are many family members depicted over many generations.

On one end of the room is a platform, or rather a stage, where two oversized thrones are centered. Covered in scarlet red velvet, the chairs show prominence, class, and distinction. They are clearly for the leaders of the town, namely the king and his queen. Also balancing the space, there are two small sets of stairs that both rise up on opposite sides of the stage, leading up to the two thrones.

In one corner and partially hidden from view, behind the magistrate's thrones, is a staircase leading up to another floor of the castle. Just like the stairs leading from the main room to Amiranda's bedroom, the top of this staircase remains unseen from view from the lower level.

Positioned at the room's entry, a uniformed royal guard stands at attention, securing the doorway. He stands with his back against the wall, next to a door that far more resembles a drawbridge than a normal door. For protection, he is wearing a full bodysuit made of shining armor, with a matching helmet covering his head. The royal guard's helmet has a hinged visor to shield and protect his eyes when in battle; even though everyone knows that the town of Luxing has never seen a real battle before nor probably ever will. In one hand, the royal guard supports a long battle-axe, while in the other there is a large gold trumpet. The elongated trumpet is neatly adorned with a yellow and purple flag draping down from its long and narrow stem.

As is customary, the guard blows the horn to announce someone's presence or to get the people's attention when the king has an important announcement to make. Although serving little real purpose, his presence is deemed necessary to protect the royal family, specifically the king who is working nearby at his desk.

The magistrate's noble desk is exaggeratedlyy oversized and rests on the main level of the ballroom, just in front of the platform and the overseer's thrones. Its prominent size dramatically reflects the ruler's importance and grandeur. The king sits hunched over the many papers that are awaiting his feathered pen's approval. He signs his name on each one after he diligently looks them over.

The royal overseer is a rather chubby man, not tall in stature, but his firm conduct and noble stage presence more than make up for these "shortcomings." Exhibiting his royalty, the king is wearing an exquisite crown atop his head. The crown is made of pure gold and rich jewels, which both shimmer and shine in the soft light of the room.

To add to his prominence, King Jedrek is also wearing a blue velvet robe—a robe that drapes all the way down to the floor. Since it is impossible to see his feet when in motion, it appears as if the king is floating whenever he walks. There are bands of white ruffling fur around the robe's collar and cuffs, quite commonly traditional of a king's royal garment.

The ruler's short and stocky appearance combined with his royal gown, his long white and flowing beard, and matching moustache, make him somewhat resemble a short but harsh St. Nicholas of olden times. However, he is not as plump as Santa Claus—and far from being nearly as jolly.

Three short, quick knocks are heard at the door.

"Who is it?" asks the guard, in a heavy and very whining English accent. He persistently remains standing at full attention at the door, positioned with his back against the wall. At all times, the guard is looking straightforward ahead as a true soldier ought.

"Why it's me again sir," replies the voice behind the door. The voice carries a similar yet different, distinct and whiny English accent.

"Just what I need," the king sarcastically exclaims to himself, overhearing the voice outside. "Tell him I'm busy," he tells the guard. Industriously, the king continues working, looking over his many papers and inking them with his feathered pen.

"The eminent King Jedrek of Luxing is busy now; come back later," the royal guard announces through the door.

"I'll only be but a moment your highness," squalls the man from the other side.

Yule, the guard, seeks direction from his majesty. "Shall I allow him in, Sire?" he asks.

The king signs one last paper before looking at the large stacks of documents that will soon follow. Although he has toiled for hours, he has only completed a small portion of his work. He waits for a moment, and then shakes his head, realizing that the man from behind the door will never allow him to finish, not at least without further interruption.

"Yes, Yule," the king replies reluctantly, "let him in."

The royal guard raises the hinged visor of his helmet. Still holding his battle-axe at attention by his side, Yule lifts his royal trumpet, triumphantly blowing the gold instrument with great fanfare. It is quite a display of showmanship, considering that there are only two people in the room—the king and the royal guard himself. Still, it is customary.

Comically, the guard's visor is too loose and falls right on the horn's mouthpiece, abruptly interrupting the royal guard's playing. With a loud crash, it slams down—*Clunk!* He quickly props his squeaky visor back up.

"Hear ye, Hear ye," Yule announces, broadcasting his whining voice aloud for all to hear, yet there is no one else around. "Your majesty, may I present the royal court jester, Sir Roxen, *formerly of Worthington....*"

The royal guard opens the door. There stands a rather tall, skinny, and quite awkward-looking man. The odd man is wearing a ridiculous brightly colored red and green court jester suit which makes him look more like an elf than any other ordinary human. Roxen's jester outfit is outlandishly decorated, complete with a four-pointed hat that droops over his head and sometimes blocks his view.

To add to the absurdity, Roxen is wearing green overly taut tights, a jester's kilt, and gnome-like shoes which curl up at the toes. Bells are attached to each one of the pointy tips of the performer's hat and shoes. Whenever he moves, the bells jingle in direct correlation to his comedic movements. Loosely wrapped and hanging around his waist, Roxen has a leather satchel in which to carry some of his gear. The entertainer proudly walks in carrying his court jester stick, grinning merrily from ear to ear.

Yule welcomes him in. "Cheerio once again, my good man," he says, for once turning his head to greet the man.

"Cheerio, Yule," Roxen replies to his comrade; "how's the wife ol' chap?" The two talk jovially with one another, having met many times before under the same circumstances.

"Bloody expensive, I tell you." Yule begins talking one on one with his English pal, absentmindedly forgetting the king's presence. He breaks off all formal precautions of security and relaxes to talk to his old friend.

"With all the money that she spends, why she nearly costs me a king's ransom," he continues. The royal guard carries on his conversation with the court jester intimately, but soon realizes the badly chosen analogy made in front of his royal eminence.

Yule quickly excuses himself, "Ahem, oh, quite sorry Sire." Once again, he props himself upright against the wall, standing firmly at attention. Comically on cue, his visor slams down once again—*Thunk!*

"What can I do for you today, Roxen?" the king asks as he looks up momentarily. He immediately resumes his paperwork, hoping to get a little work done, at least for the moment. It is perfectly clear that the king is a very stern man who does not have time for anything having no direct relation to business, especially meaningless banter, and he *never* laughs.

Meanwhile, unbeknownst to all, the men's conversation is not private. Having overheard the loud fanfare of Yule's trumpet, Amiranda has crept down the first couple of steps of the staircase, careful not to be seen or heard. She is only curious to see who is here, as no one was expecting any visitors or guests today. She does not mean to pry, as that would be improper and against her father's orders, but she cannot contain her curiosity. The young princess sits near the top of the staircase on the highest step she can, where she can still be out of sight. She is cradling

Peatie as always.

Amiranda softly whispers alone to Peatie, "Oh Peatie, our friend Roxen is here!" She tightly embraces her pup, anxiously awaiting the court jester's humor and pleasantries. "How he does amuse me. Let's see what tricks he does for us this time."

In the meantime, the conversation between Roxen and the king continues....

"I return once again seeking a position under your magistrate, your magistrate," Roxen announces, ridiculously repeating himself. He kindly takes a bow before the king, benevolently sweeping his arm across his waist as a form of goodwill and a gesture of respect.

"A job?" the king emphatically repeats, amused by the court jester's eager persistence. "Haven't we been over this a thousand times?" he retorts loudly, looking up for the moment once again. "There is simply no place under my jurisdiction for someone like you."

Roxen pleads back to the king, "But I'm a court jester, Sire. I am supposed to work for a king of assuming position—someone admirable, someone of excellence, someone like you."

However sincere Roxen's request may be, the jester's endeavor is not at all taken seriously.

"Why don't you try to get work from some other king?" the king replies sarcastically, "perhaps *Worthington*."

Yule props up his visor, which squeaks each time it moves. "But Sire," he says, in his same and usual high tone of voice, "they haven't got a king." His visor slams down just as he finishes speaking—*Clank!*

"Then perhaps try somewhere else," the king growls back, growing even more agitated. Having already wasted much of his precious time, the king returns to his paperwork, shuffling his papers around almost aimlessly.

Yule steps forward, raising his visor and interjecting once again.

"But Sire, there aren't any other kings," he points out, showing some support for his dear old friend. This time, and to everyone's amazement, his visor remains propped up for a second. Just when they all think it is going to stay in place, it slams shut—*Slam!* Yule has no choice but to retreat. He cautiously steps back into place, his back pressed almost dead against the wall. The royal guard's statement is totally unnecessary due to the well-known fact of the matter.

By now, King Jedrek is turning bright red in the face, angered by the persistence of both men. It has become increasingly self-evident that the king's blood pressure is steadily rising. His patience is also wearing thinner and thinner with each and every moment he is kept from his obligatory duties.

"Yule!" the king shouts to the royal guard with great sternness in his voice. Everyone can easily tell that by no means does he want to further encourage the already overzealous jester.

"Sorry Sire." Yule replies. His voice is muffled, echoing within the confines of his covered helmet. He props it open once more. This time it remains lifted as Yule keeps his own mouth shut.

"Now Roxen, what ever did happen to good ol' *King Worthington*?" The king smirks cleverly.

A pin drop can be heard as Roxen attempts to think of a reply that would be appropriate, given both the seriousness of the situation and the reality of the matter. Made uneasy by this inquiry, the court jester becomes very fidgety in his movements. He knows that the king must have at least somewhat heard what had occurred there, the old kingdom of Worthington being not so far away from the kingdom of Luxing. Small beads of sweat begin to trickle down his upper brow. His broad wide grin lessens as he quickly realizes that rumors surely must have spread throughout the entire kingdom by now.

After a moment's deliberation, the jester finally stutters a reply, nervously loosening his collar at the same time. "Well he kind of had a … well a sort of … mishap … the poor soul."

Yule whines, "A mishap?" *Slam!* His visor shuts once more.

Slowly, the king leans forward. For once he is entirely disregarding any sort of business to which he should be attending and paying all the more attention to the court jester. King Jedrek has the insatiable curiosity to hear Roxen's version of what actually transpired, or rather his tale of the story, especially after a long, hard day of work. Perhaps the court jester's presence will certainly amuse the king after all. Plus, it gives the king great pleasure to put the jester at further unease.

"What kind of, sort of, mishap, Roxen?" he asks. At the same time the king is mildly mocking the jester, he is mindful to not become too overly apparent, asking his question almost respectfully, out of mere curiosity. Yule carefully props up his pesky visor once again, letting out a slight, almost unnoticeable squeak.

"Well, I don't quite bloody well know what happened precisely; but the fire didn't totally disintegrate the entire castle—it being made of stone and all," Roxen explains, shrugging his shoulders at the very end of his reply. He sporadically makes eye contact with his majesty, cautious not to divulge too much information.

"I don't want to know," the king finally replies, sorry he asked.

Roxen tries to digress and change the subject. "I've learned more tricks, Sire. Most of them having nothing to do with fire at all; that is, ever since the incident." The jester's words become increasingly muffled as he speaks of the fire and the occurrence about which he would rather not mention.

Amiranda, still listening from atop the stairs, begins to giggle. Quickly she cups her hand to her mouth. Still, she is careful not to be heard.

Yule interjects once again. "Oh do show, jolly good chap," he tells Roxen, enthused and intrigued by his friend's new and never-seen-before talents. The king looks at the guard in sheer disbelief; his eyes piercing right though him. Yule looks around, first to the king, then to the court jester and then back at the king. He is shocked that his visor for once remained in the upright position. Knowing he should have kept his mouth shut, Yule willingly slams down his own visor. *Clunk!*

Roxen continues, "Allow me to get some of my props."

Enthusiastically the jester exits the door, leaving it partially open so that he can reenter. A huge ruckus is heard just outside the doorway: the clanking of some metal utensils, quick piping of a piccolo, the squeal of a cat, and the squeaking of a child's toy all clamor humorously. Lastly the sound of a large metal cylinder is heard falling and then rolling around, creating a huge disturbance; eventually it settles in the distance.

Yule's facial expressions alter in direct correlation to the diverse sounds—puzzlement, amusement, apprehension, and ultimately a painful twinge as he hears the loud crash coming from behind the door. The king places his hand firmly against his forehead, shaking his head in sheer disbelief. One would think he would be used to all this by now.

Roxen rushes back in immediately, only this time he is riding on a miniature tricycle. One by one, he throws five different colored balls into the air, juggles them, while at the same time humming and whistling a catchy tune. With great speed the jester whizzes around the room, swiftly circling around the king, thus clumsily spinning the king around in his royal chair. The king's many important papers go flying every which way across the room. Everything is a mess.

Cycling frantically, Roxen runs over the documents, marking each one of the papers with skid marks made from his tricycle. If that is not bad enough, lastly, as a grand finale, the jester tosses each one of his juggling balls high up into the air. Just as the king slowly stops spinning in his chair, one by one the balls fall onto the king's head. Each one falls and sounds with a great thump. The only exception is the very last ball that the court jester catches firmly in his mouth. It is like a scene or act taken from some sort of cabaret show—a very bad one.

Still unseen, Amiranda and her pup are amused by the court jester's zany antics. Amiranda smiles and does her best not to laugh aloud. Luckily, the two of them remain unheard.

"That's pretty good, Roxen," the king dizzily remarks.

Slowly, King Jedrek rises from his chair. Calmly he walks from behind his desk and around to the front of it. He approaches the young court jester, heading toward him nonchalantly. Yule is amazed by how well the king is reacting and behaving. Roxen is beaming from ear to ear, resting on one knee with both arms spread out as if to say "Tada!"

Breathing heavily through his nose, Roxen rests for a second to try and catch his breath, the juggling ball stuck firmly in his mouth. It is as if he is waiting for the king's approval, trying hard to make it look like the performance comes so naturally and easy to him when in fact it is a hard act to follow.

The jester is disheveled from the performance—a performance worthy enough for some sort of award, although there will not be any, at least not for today.

The king kindly puts his arm around Roxen as if to commend him for a job well done. He leisurely hesitates for just a moment, allowing the happy jester to soak in the glory of the moment. Roxen is truly proud for putting on such a great show. In his mind, he has gotten the job hands down.

Then, suddenly, with one swift motion, King Jedrek pats or rather hits Roxen square on his back. Uncontrollably, the jester swallows the ball. You can see the faint protrusion of the ball as it heads down the jester's throat and into his belly. Unable to take any more abuse, the king finally lets out a huge scream. "NOW GET OUT!" he yells.

"But I'm not quite done yet," Roxen remarks, now having fully swallowed the ball.

"Out, OUT, O-U-T!" The king yells, his command growing louder each time he repeats it. The king's yelling practically pushes Roxen toward the door.

Now begging, the court jester pleads to him, "but you haven't even seen my pet elephant trick yet." Right on cue, an elephant's blare is heard outside in the hallway.

"Jolly good show, me ol' chap," Yule confirms to the jester privately, praising his dear friend while having to escort him out at the same time. Roxen smiles back graciously.

In the doorway, Roxen confidentially tells Yule, "Work on him for me won't you, my good fellow. I think I'm finally getting through to him." Yule nods his head while gently pushing him out the door, as he cannot let friendship stand in the way of his royal duties. "Good day now

Sire," Roxen says to the king out loud.

The king, flustered by all of the shenanigans taking place in his palace, lets out one last plea for some sanity from all of this madness.

"For the last time, GET OUT!" he screams. The king's scream is so loud that it slams the door shut while at the same time it also slams down Yule's visor. All of Roxen's props and accessories can be heard outside falling and crashing—as if some have fallen down a flight of stairs.

Softly, the king exclaims to himself, "How did he ever get that elephant into my castle?" He shakes his head in disbelief.

Still unseen and unheard, Amiranda giggles at the top of the stairs.

With the royal papers still spread out everywhere across the room, Yule aids the king as they make a feeble attempt to salvage them. Most of them are now tousled and torn, casualties of the court jester and his crazy antics. Quickly, they pick them up from off the floor in great large heaps.

"Where does he come up with these half-brained schemes?" King Jedrek asks himself. "I'm trying to run a castle here, not some sort of circus," he continues, still somewhat in disbelief.

The king sits back down at the desk in order to reorganize, resort, and salvage some of the papers. He places them neatly together, patting the edges of each bundle firmly against the desk trying to straighten them.

Relieved to be alone again, he heaves a heavy sigh, anxious to return to the business at hand. For a moment, all is quiet.

Chapter 6

Doctor's Orders

Another knock is heard at the door. This time there are three soft, light taps.

"What is it now, Roxen?" the king reluctantly asks.

The door opens, but it is not the court jester as the king predicted. Instead, in the entranceway is someone else, someone unexpected—the king's personal family physician.

The doctor is an older gentleman, skinny and of average height, and is balding with what is left of his hair just starting to turn gray. Dressed in the same kind of attire that a typical doctor would have, he is wearing a long white medical coat that reaches down just past his knees. Just below the coat one can see his brown-colored slacks and his slightly darker brown leather shoes. To aid him with his vision, the doc has his reading glasses on, which make him look both intelligent and sophisticated, like the professional he is. At his side, the physician is holding a black leather medical bag—apparently full of his medical equipment. A stethoscope is neatly draped around his neck, a necessity for any physician in the medical field.

Yule stands upright at attention, ready to announce the doctor's arrival. "Hear ye, Hear ye," he broadcasts, again as if there are many in the room. The king interrupts the announcement with a definitive, throat-clearing "Ahem." Amiranda remains watching diligently from the top of the stairs.

"Oh, good afternoon Doc," the king remarks; he is ever so thankful that it is not the crazed jester returning. The king hesitates for a moment, appearing a bit perplexed, still trying to figure out the reason for the doctor's visit. "But, if I'm not mistaken, I just had my checkup last week," he admits.

The doctor hesitates for a moment, allowing the severity of the matter sink in, as there is an important reason why he is here. In a sincere tone of voice he replies, "I'm not here to see you. I mean, not for a physical that is. I am afraid that I have some bad news."

The doctor, still partially in the doorway, takes one step closer toward his royal highness. Almost instantly, the feel of the room drastically changes from being carefree and aloof, as when Roxen was performing, to serious and somber.

"Yule, will you excuse us?" the king requests, speaking with the same seriousness as exhibited by the doctor.

"As you wish my Sire." Yule steps outside and closes the door behind him.

King Jedrek and the doctor are now all alone, with the exception of Amiranda and her dog Peatie who are still unseen at the top of the staircase. Amiranda did not originally come as an eavesdropper, but only to see the royal court jester perform. Now, intrigued by the physician's visit, she cannot bear to turn away—which is especially risky now that everything is quiet, the more likely it is that she could be caught. Amiranda has no choice but to stay.

The dialogue between the two men continues....

"What is it Doc?" the king asks emphatically.

The doctor gets right to the point. "I'm afraid that your daughter's nanny is very sick; and there's not much that I can do for her." The doctor's words are quite sorrowful, yet still professional given his gentle and practiced bedside manner. Although he maintains good eye contact with the king, the physician frequently looks down at the ground as he tries to envision not only the right words to say, but the right way to say them.

Amiranda looks onward, terrified. She is quite worried about her Nana's condition. The princess holds her pup tightly, in an attempt to hold back the tears that are beginning to well up in her eyes. Peatie also shows great compassion, seeming to be aware of what Amiranda is feeling.

The doctor continues, "It seems as though she has caught some strange, rare ailment that simply cannot be cured. Not without the proper remedy, that is. I have her resting in bed for now, but realize that there is not much time to get her the medicine she needs." He is very solemn as he speaks, showing the gravity of the matter.

Hearing the doctor's words, Amiranda squeezes her pup even tighter than before—clinging to him ever so closely. A solitary tear falls from her eye, one that softly escaped, regardless of how hard she tried not to let it. Quickly, she wipes it away with the tip of her finger, careful not to let herself cry. A sudden silence fills the room.

Although the king is well known throughout the land to be a rather stern and uncompassionate man, for once he shows a very different side of himself. He is quite genuinely concerned for Amiranda's caregiver.

"Well what can we do?" he asks. "Let's get her the medication." King Jedrek answers his own question, insisting on a simple solution. After all, he is used to giving orders and having them followed without question.

"I'm afraid it's not that simple," Doc explains, this time looking directly at the king. "I've only heard of one other incidence of a cure for what she has, and that was done by the man they call the '*Savant*.'" The doctor pauses before continuing. "It is said that he lives in the Deciduous Forest from what tales I have heard—that is if he is still even alive there."

The physician's reply is rather mysterious, especially considering that it is coming from someone who is a man of practical medicine.

"Well, can't we get someone to go there to find this man?" the king asks, still insistent that he could easily amend things.

"I'm sorry your majesty," the doctor apologizes. "I'm afraid it's not that simple. You know of all the tales about the Deciduous Forest. I cannot find a man willing to face such danger," he explains.

King Jedrek, overly accustomed to definitive ruling, makes a decision. "I will put out a bulletin—the highest reward to the person who brings me back this man they call the Savant." It is clear that he is proud of his executive resolution of the matter.

"Very well your highness, as you wish. Good day to you." The doctor bids farewell and bows his head partway down, knowing that the king's solution to the problem is improbable at best.

"Thank you Doc," the king tells him before returning to his papers at hand. "And, oh yes," he is suddenly reminded; "not a word to Amiranda. It would upset her terribly." The doctor leaves and closes the door. The king goes about his royal business as usual.

Amiranda, having heard the whole conversation, has clearly shed a few tears by now. Still, she remains strong. For one, she knows that she must. Secondly, she has no other choice. Most importantly, she knows very well in her mind what she has to do.

Softly she whispers, "Nana will be okay Peatie, don't worry." The princess calmly strokes the delicate fur on his head to console the pup, but perhaps more so for her own comfort. "We'll get her help," she states with equal amounts of determination and uncertainty in her voice.

Amiranda stands up, all the while holding her pup, careful not to make a noise. Mistakably, Peatie lets out a small whimper—almost loud enough for her father to hear.

At first, the king is unsure what to make of the sound.

"Hello, is someone up there?" he calls out to the top of the staircase. Amiranda remains there motionless, fearful her father will discover her and find her there listening. In her mind she swears that he can hear her heart rhythmically beating, giving her away. She holds Peatie's face closely to her chest to both silence and calm him.

After a moment, the king, satisfied that the noise is either the creaking of the castle settling, or maybe a mouse, or perhaps even that he is beginning to hear things, diligently returns to his work. Quietly, Amiranda tiptoes back to her room undetected.

Chapter 7

No Time for Sorrow

Lying face down on her bed, Amiranda softly cries into her pillow. The young princess is trying hard not to let her emotions get to her. It is now midafternoon, with the sun reaching near the tops of the trees in the distance. Birds sing joyously outside, yet Amiranda's heart is heavy.

Peatie, who always remains at the princess' side, pries himself gently from her arms, pulling himself closer to her face. He nudges her softly as if longing to be petted, but more so just to give her the comfort she needs and to keep her company in her time of sadness. The two of them lie there, nearly motionless, except for their gentle breathing. For them, time passes ever so slowly.

Far too upset to rest, Amiranda props herself upright at the foot of her bed and wipes one last tear away with her finger. She picks up Peatie's brush and softly runs the bristles through his fur, while she is still trying to hold back more tears.

"Oh Peatie, there must be something we can do," she tells him, coaxing his fur softly. "There must be some way we can get Nana the help she so desperately needs." Amiranda is visibly overcome with fear, not only fear for her own self, but also fear for her Nana's welfare.

"Why I don't know what I would ever do if something ever happened to her. *I don't know what any of us would do.* She is the only one holding this family together; why if something happened to her …"

Amiranda stops midsentence, realizing the truth of her statement as well as all of the consequences that would take place if something unexpected were to happen to her nanny. Forcefully, the princess pulls herself back together. She knows that this is a time for her to be strong, and most of all, not to give up.

The princess carries her young pup over to the window, still cradling him in her arms for protection. "Peatie," she tells him, "we have to try to help Nana. We have to find this Savant—and try to get the cure for her. He's the only one who can help us," she whispers, gazing out her window to the late day sky. Amiranda is absolute in her words and passionate in her heart.

She looks across the pond, beyond the meadow, and out to the tips of the trees that make up the Deciduous Forest—the same dark forest so mysteriously hushed by everyone, for every time someone begins to mention the forest, the very same people quickly change the subject because of the forbidden nature of the topic. It is as though the very mention of the forest itself is considered somewhat taboo and most unwelcome ... *especially* in Amiranda's kingdom of Luxing.

Though the land surrounding the forest is incredibly vibrant and alive, the interior of the forest appears dark and ominous, with strange, dark billowing clouds constantly looming overhead. The same late day sun that seems to illuminate all the land around the forest casts a deep shadow within it.

"… It's up to you and me now," the young princess sighs.

Chapter 8

Beginning the Quest

It is late in the day, almost nightfall, not an appropriate time for anyone to make such a perilous journey. Still, Amiranda knows what she has to do and she is determined to go through with her plan. So, despite the time of day, she takes her pup Peatie and her parrot Reynolds along on her journey.

Wearing only a pale yellow sundress, which is neatly trimmed with a pale blue ribbon around the waistline and her collar, the princess is not dressed appropriately for such a daring venture. It is attire more fitting for a short summer day's outing than a long trip through the woods, and her outfit very much resembles a comfortable yet delicate nightgown, like the ones she usually wears. Nevertheless, Amiranda leads the way.

Steadily the three make their way toward the forest, through the field that lies immediately behind the castle—the same field that can be seen from both Amiranda's bedroom window and the rec room that lies directly below hers. Amiranda and Peatie walk along a naturally made dirt trail that leads almost straight to the forest while Reynolds flies overhead.

Peatie is trailing behind Amiranda, constantly tripping at her feet, playfully running along in order to try and keep up. He is carefree and joyous to be running around outside for a change. Reynolds flies ahead and then trails behind, in order to compensate for his aerial speed. Being domesticated, he is far from being the brave and adventurous type, and does not stray too far ahead or fall too far behind.

Amiranda walks steadily, carrying with her only a homemade traveling pouch containing some bare necessities for her and her two pets. Made from a broomstick handle, which she found in the downstairs closet, and one of her pillowcases neatly tied to one end of it, some of the pouch's contents can be seen peeking out. Resting the long end of the stick over her shoulder for support, the princess diligently lugs the pouch along.

The trail is slightly curved, shaped almost like the letter "S." It first heads to the right, then to the left, and then finally to the right again—making its way around the pond, then around the hilly part of the meadow, and finally into the forest. Rows and rows of brilliantly colored wildflowers border each side of the trail, which is quite picturesque in and of itself. Adding to the grand beauty of the day, an impressive fiery, purple-red sky shines majestically over the pond and field. However magnificent the late day may be, there, looming in the distance, lies the darkness that has already settled over the Deciduous Forest.

The forest is a deep, dark, and shadowy bluish green. So dark in fact, that all traces of color totally disappear the farther you look into the woods. Shades of blue-black and gray-black slowly fade into a deep, dark black-black. The darkness envelops the woods, making it look both ominous and unsettling, perhaps conveying a warning sign to Amiranda. However, having little experience with such matters, the princess continues onward, thinking nothing of the dangers that may lie ahead.

About one quarter of the way along the trail, at the edge of the pond, Amiranda and her friends stop for a moment. All of spring's wondrous and colorful flowers are fully in bloom. Their sweet fragrance fills the air with a breathtaking aroma as each blossom appears as though it was painstakingly hand-painted by Mother Nature herself.

As Amiranda looks around the pond, the more she sees that all life around it is very animate and *alive*. There are a countless number of lily pads floating on the pond's surface, with each cluster adorning their very own flowering water lilies. She watches the hummingbirds as they hover perfectly in midair, the chipmunks coming to take a drink from the pond, and even the bees gathering nectar from the limitless supply of flowers. Frogs curiously leap from one pad to another with ease, and many different varieties of birds splash about; they are cleansing themselves while playing in the life-giving water. Now that winter has ended and spring has begun, it seems as if all of nature is here at the pond. In addition, they are all excited and eager to enjoy the season's rich blessing. That is, *almost* everyone.

The princess remains there at the water's edge, mesmerized by all that is around her, mystically gazing into her own reflection created on the pond's surface. Just beneath the water, Amiranda sees a small school of fish swimming around happily. She thinks to herself, how fully content they are, not really needing anything except one another.

Amiranda gently places her carry-along bag down on the ground beside her, partially opening the pouch, careful not to let its contents spill out. Out from her pillowcase, the princess pulls a small glass jar partially filled with water. She closes up the sack and holds the glass jar up, close to her eye, looking inside.

Inside the jar swims her pet goldfish, Molly. Amiranda peers deep inside the jar, watching carefully as she swims around nearly motionless, confined by the narrow walls of the glass container. The two look at one another, both unsure of the other's future. It was only earlier today that the princess realized the loneliness her pet has long endured, much like her own loneliness inside. She hopes that it is not too late to correct it.

Kneeling at the water's edge, Amiranda slowly twists and releases the cork off the jar. The tall grass reeds of the pond surround her, gently blowing in the wind. She brushes her hair away from her eyes, combing it with her hands, and placing part of it over her ears. Cautiously, she places the entire jar in the water, upright so that the glass walls of the container are surrounded by Molly's soon to be new environment.

The small fish looks around. She is anxious, terrified, and unsettled about the new world that has been placed before her. Undoubtedly, Amiranda shares the same feelings. Molly sees the other fish examining her, the way school kids would carefully examine and scrutinize a new student. They are all very different from her—fish of different sizes, different colors, different types; even different groupings. It is the classic case of the proverbial small fish in a large pond.

The lone fish looks once more at Amiranda, this time up from out of the glass enclosure. Decisively yet gradually, the princess gently tips the jar, allowing the pond's water to slowly enter. The two waters mix into one.

The school of fish looks onward as Molly hesitates for her departure. In her heart she knows that this is the end of one existence and perhaps the start of another, God willing.

Without looking back and unexpectedly in a sudden gust of glory, Molly darts out of the glass jar. She shoots off like an arrow, headfirst straight into the pond. Amiranda hopes that this act of quickly leaving was a promising decision to make the best of her new life, and not an irreverent good-bye. Slowly Molly disappears with the other fish deep into the water, not to be seen again.

Amiranda looks into the still waters, unable to see any more fish. Perhaps all were spooked by the glass jar, the princess herself, or the sudden commotion of a new fish entering. Nonetheless, the princess is still worried for her friend, but knows in her heart that she has made the right decision; it was time to let her go. Quietly and reverently, Amiranda sings to her small aquatic friend, as if Molly is still somehow able to hear her ...

Sometimes friends
Have to part,
But you know you
You're in my heart.

And when life
Has to change,
You know my love
Will be the same.

Seasons come and go so fast;
We both know time will never last.
We've both grown and come to know
There's no easy way in letting go.

Sometimes change
Comes your way,
And you will have to
Find your way.

Through the pain
And the tears,
Know that I will
Always be here.

Now it's time
For us to part,
But there's just no easy part
For us in letting go, letting go....

Besides Amiranda's singing, not a word was said. Truth is, Amiranda didn't know what to say—she did not know how to say good-bye. In fact, part of her did not want to say good-bye. Then again, come to think of it, no words were needed. Both the princess and her pet goldfish knew each other's full thoughts and emotions as both were in the same exact predicament. Both were encased by the stone and glass walls in which they lived.

A stray tear gently falls down Amiranda's cheek; Peatie kindly licks it away. The princess already misses her dear friend and thinks to herself about how she would hate to lose her nanny too. Now, ever more determined, she immediately pulls herself up off the ground; she shows strength, courage and conviction once again.

"C'mon guys," she says; "we've got work to do...."

The sun is starting to set as the unique trio of friends head down the trail, making their way through the field. Gradually they begin to enter the woods. One can almost see the untold number of wandering eyes gazing upon them as they proceed into the strange, dark, and ominous Deciduous Forest.

Chapter 9

The Forest

It is dark now as the three proceed much more slowly and far more cautiously into the shadowy forest. Slender beams of moonlight dimly stream through the few small holes in the forest's canopy, somewhat lighting and leading the travelers on the narrow and winding trail. The moon plays tricks of images with their many silhouettes—shadows cast by the light flickering through the swaying tree branches above. The forest's crooked and decrepit looking branches make it appear as though strange figures are moving about with every slight breeze. Amiranda and her friends have the eerie feeling they are being watched.

Even though it is springtime, the forest itself appears to be mostly dormant and very inanimate—quite unusual for this time of year. It almost seems as though time has erratically stopped within the forest's boundaries. Oddly, it feels like an unnatural, eternal autumn has settled throughout the woods. The branches are barren of leaves, lifeless, and empty. On those branches that do have leaves, the leaves are all dry, brown, and shriveled up.

Most of the trees are well aged; they are large and rugged, soaring straight to the sky—as the forest has remained left alone, unchanged, and avoided for many years. The only exception is the small amount of adolescent trees that have somehow managed to sparsely grow here and there throughout the woodlands. For some inexplicable reason, the forest remains abnormally and eerily quiet—void of any animal noises. All one can sense is the sound of the wind whistling in the trees and the feel of the cold chill filling the air.

The princess and her friends continue for what seems like hours. The three of them are now deep in the woods, making their way farther along the winding trail. As far as Amiranda is concerned, there is no turning back. Reynolds is flying much closer now, careful not to go too far away from the princess and her pup. Leaves rustle and twigs crackle beneath their feet with every step they take. Constantly they look around them, forever scanning the wilderness, weary of everything. As the night grows even darker, they all walk even slower, their own shadows steadily following each one of them.

Suddenly, they hear something move in the brush, coming from a small hill just to the left of them. In an instant they all halt, standing motionless in their very own footsteps. Reynolds lands directly behind Amiranda, displaying his cowardliness toward the strange and mysterious noise.

Amiranda silences the two. "Shhh," she exclaims softly. "What was that?" she immediately asks. No one dares make a peep.

All is eerily silent for the moment. The group looks on guardedly as no one dares to make a move. In fact, they hardly even take one breath. The rustling is heard once again.

Inquisitively and somewhat courageously, Peatie barks at the strange noise with a high-pitched yelp. Although small, the young pup shows that he would eagerly offer his protection toward his kind mistress if need be.

Reynolds echoes, "What was that? Arrk, what was that?" They all remain motionless.

Once again the dense, shadowy brush mysteriously rustles—first here, then there, then over there. They turn their heads quickly in unison, following the strange sound as it wanders in the leaves and brush. They all remain especially close together, maintaining their strength as a unit. They are also careful to stay under a fairly well lit part of the path, prepared to respond to the unknown.

Unexpectedly, and much to their surprise, a small round object comes rolling directly toward them. They are not able to get a good look at exactly what it is, but from the looks of it, it resembles an old boulder rolling end over end—dark green, round and splotchy. It speeds out of the woodland's brush, spinning uncontrollably right toward the traveling wanderers.

Startled by the strange oddity, Amiranda and her two companions swiftly jump out of its way. The princess could have sworn she heard the object yelling as it was about to collide with her. Rolling swiftly, it barely misses Amiranda's leg, but instead hits the trunk of a large oak tree, which is directly behind her. Amiranda quickly turns around, trying to get a visual.

"What was that?" she asks wondering. The jolt of the impact abruptly stops the mysterious entity dead in its tracks. It thumps to a halt.

At first Amiranda does not know what to make of the strange creature. She realizes that it must be alive, having been able to hear it, but it is too dark to tell what it possibly could be. Peatie yelps at the intruder to both investigate and to ward it off. Now immobilized by the crash, it becomes apparent to them that the object is actually a turtle's shell, which they can barely see in the dim light.

Peatie carefully inspects the unexpected visitor, cautiously sniffing the animal's naturally made armor. From within the round shell a turtle's head suddenly pops out. The unexpected transformation startles the small pup. Peatie backs up immediately but continues to yelp.

"I thought I told you to look where you're going," a voice calls, heard still within the shell.

Clearly perplexed by the strange remark made by the turtle, Peatie immediately stops barking. He does not know what to make of the outlandish creature, nor do the others. No one ever heard of a talking turtle before, let alone seen one. Amiranda takes one step closer in order to look and examine it. Without warning, another head pops out from the same shell. The princess gasps, surprised that there are now two turtle's heads, both of which are talking.

"Me?" exclaims the other turtle's head. "Well if it weren't for your bad directions we never would have gotten lost in the first place," he says firmly.

The two turtle's heads both peer up at the three strangers. "Please excuse Sigmund, he was never quite taught any manners," says the politer of the two, truly apologetic for his discourteous companion.

Amiranda is taken off guard by the strange creature. "You t—alk ..." she says, quite incredulously.

"Ah, get off my back Simon!" Sigmund, the feisty turtle retorts to his far more civil counterpart.

Although the two turtles share one common shell, they are very individualistic in personality, which clearly makes it problematic for the two of them. Sigmund and Simon both have to agree on everyday simple tasks like where to go, how to get there, and what to do. Since both share and control a common set of limbs, this often causes a power struggle between the two. Simply put, if they do not agree on something, it literally gets them nowhere.

To add to the two turtle's shortcomings, both turtles, or rather turtle heads, have quite opposite personalities or quirks about them. On one side, Simon is well learned. As if he came from an academic background, he seems very high-cultured and he has a well-spoken voice. Sigmund, on the other hand, has a raspier, much harsher voice. He talks just like his name sounds—*Sigmund.*

The two habitually argue with one another, having to put up with each other day after day after day. In other words, they are the "odd couple" of the forest world—both sharing the same home residence, their shell.

After a moment's quarrel between the two turtles, their dialogue continues....

"Well now that you know our names—may I ask whom I am addressing?" Simon, the brighter of the two turtles addresses the trio, showing his sociability toward Amiranda and her friends. He speaks very courteously to her, unlike Sigmund who, on the other hand, is well, far unlike Simon.

"Y—ou t—talk," Amiranda repeats herself, stuttering once again. This time, however, one can almost understand her.

"My, isn't she a real conversationalist," Sigmund remarks sarcastically. For some unknown reason Sigmund seems greatly disgruntled, not wanting to have anything to do with her, or anyone else for that matter. His gruff voice adds to his apparent inhospitality.

"My, that *is* a big word for you, Sigmund," Simon says back to him. "Now let the lady have a word for a moment, you babbling nitwit." Once again Simon apologizes for his sibling's rude behavior, before politely urging Amiranda to continue. "I'm sorry my dear, what were you saying?"

The three travelers all look at one another, still partially frozen in disbelief. Amiranda is hesitant to reply, not knowing what to say. Is she dreaming? She has talked to animals before, but with the exception of her parrot, who only repeats what others have said, no other animal has ever talked back to her before using their own language. Apprehensively, she decides to satisfy her curiosity.

"Oh," the princess replies, "My name is Amiranda." She takes a deep breath, hesitating for a second before continuing. "This is my dog, Peatie, and my parrot, Reynolds." Amiranda kindly gestures to her two animal companions, still unsure if it is her imagination running wild.

Reynolds squawks a warm "Hello" as he has been taught how to say it so well. Peatie starts sniffing around, trying to check the turtles out, while still maintaining a safe distance out of harm's way, just in case.

The animals' interaction toward one another partially convinces the princess that this is indeed real, or at least for now she plays along with her dream. "Nice to make your acquaintance," Amiranda curtsies, not knowing how to greet a two-headed talking turtle. She quickly realizes her slip-up.

"Ah, royalty," Simon declares with astonishing accuracy to his guess. He bows his head as a warm gesture of friendship and admiration.

Amiranda quickly denies the title. "No, I'm just a girl," she replies, stating in almost a wishful manner. She hopes that if she says it, it will become true, or at least she can pretend it to be, at least for now. Amiranda has spent her whole life being treated differently, and for once wants to be treated the same as any other ordinary girl. This could be her chance.

The princess regains her original train of thought. "Pardon me for asking," she respectfully excuses herself, "but how is it you two can talk?"

Peatie, still wary of the odd two-headed creature, sniffs a little closer. Amiranda picks him up, cradling him in her arms to alleviate any threat he may accidentally portray. Reynolds keeps his distance, not really trusting anyone, having to spend most of his life locked up in his cage.

"We may be slow, but we ain't stupid," Sigmund says, jumping back into the conversation with another one of his uncivilized remarks. "Ain't that right Simon?"

"That's right—*only Sigmund is both.*" Simon replies jokingly. Simon is swift at his play on words, being the quick-witted of the two. He jests with his sibling every chance that he gets.

Not realizing what Simon said at first, Sigmund quickly agrees with him. "Yeah—hey, wait a minute!" he suddenly realizes.

Amiranda lets out one of her slight giggles. "You two have been together a long time, haven't you?" She politely pretends to guess the obvious.

It is often said that twins think alike, each one knowing what the other is about to say. Sigmund and Simon are no exception, each one able to finish the other's sentence.

In answer to her question, the two turtles reply, taking turns using one word or phrase each to form a complete sentence or thought.

Simon and Sigmund alternately respond, "How long? *Fourteen years,* eight months, *sixteen long days,* and six hours precisely."

They continue, still taking turns, "We're chums," declares Sigmund. *"We're brothers,"* Simon quickly corrects. Finally both declare in unison, "And above all—*we're twins!*"

Amiranda smiles for a second, highly amused by the turtles' bizarre camaraderie. For a moment she thinks how wonderful it must be to have someone who is always there for you. After all, she is used to always being alone. That is, with the exception of having her pup and parrot as her only company. She also thinks how odd it must be to have someone know exactly what you are going to say before it has ever been said. Not even Amiranda's Nana knows the princess as well as these two know each other.

Then she suddenly realizes something of great importance to her. Having herself come from such an elite and proper upbringing, with etiquette always being of the highest importance, she is not used to the constant squabbling between the two. No one she has ever met would be allowed to carry on in such an irreverent manner. Amiranda's smile quickly diminishes, somewhat disheartened in her search to find something more to this life ...

"Well you two sure don't behave like you're related," she tells them, thinking about the way things are and the way things ought to be. "Family is supposed to be, well, *family,*" she tells them sincerely.

Amiranda is proud of her answer; how simple yet how true it should be. Her reply is not only said straightforwardly as a matter of fact, but also with a bit of tenderness, thinking back to her own family and her sick nanny. To her, this is family. And although she and her father may not be as friendly with one another as much as she would like for them to be, still, they never would quarrel like Sigmund and Simon do, as that would be undignified and inappropriate. No family should ever behave like that.

Amiranda, not letting go of her original question asks again, "You never did explain how you can talk. What I mean is, Reynolds can talk—well, kind of, but that's different."

Taking a step forward, Reynolds repeats the princess, "Reynolds can talk! Reynolds can talk! Squawk!" He extends his wings proudly, showing off.

"Truth of the matter is, we don't really know," Simon answers curiously. Being the more learned and well spoken of the two, he begins to tell the travelers a most unusual tale.

"All of the animals in the forest can talk, but not everyone can understand us," he explains to Amiranda. "Legend has it that this was brought on by a magic spell made here in the forest. It all began when a battle ignited between an evil sorcerer and a simple farmer who was working in the fields many years ago...."

Chapter 10

The Farmer and the Sorcerer

As Simon tells his story, Amiranda envisions the tale with exquisite detail and lifelike vividness. After all, the princess has stared into the forest from out of her window ever since she was a little girl. She had always realized there was something mystical—perhaps even dangerous, about the enchanted woods. Simon continues …

"Many years ago this area was a plush green meadow that spanned a great wide distance. Here lived a kind farmer with his family, a loving wife and their newborn baby boy. The man built a small house in which his family could live, unknowing that it was on the very same grounds that an evil sorcerer by the name of 'Gispan' had lost his own son in a fire years back."

During Simon's story, Amiranda pictures the images just as if she were viewing them firsthand—like in a dream that she has somehow dreamt several times before but never remembered until just now. She imagines a handsome young man plowing his field in front of his cabin. The farmer is of average height, but physically solid in his makeup and build. His shirtsleeves are rolled up over his firm forearms; his muscles are strong from the amount of exertion that hard farm work provides. He has long, light brown hair which extends from beneath his matching yet slightly darker brown leather hat.

The farmer is bent over his plow, making some mechanical adjustments to his machine. The sun is high in the sky, with the season's temperature abnormally hot due to an unexpected drought. The midsummer's heat can be seen radiating from within the dry, barren soil of the ground.

Taking a break from the midday sun, the farmer stands up and wipes a bead of perspiration away from his forehead. As he stands there looking over the field, something in the distance faintly catches his eye. Dark, ominous looking clouds billow on the horizon. The farmer turns his head toward the strange phenomenon for a better look. He is both curious and puzzled, as it is not supposed to rain for weeks due to the serious drought they are currently experiencing. Still, the sky looked far more strange and severe than any ordinary rainstorm.

The sinister-looking clouds draw nearer, slowly taking over the midday sky, covering it in an eerie darkness. In an instant, the heavens turn the deepest, darkest black, spreading outward all over the land. A dense and mysterious fog engulfs the earth all around him.

Simon pauses for a moment, which abruptly jolts the princess back to reality. Her eyes widen in amazement. Curious to hear more of the story, she asks, "Then what happened; please tell me."

Amiranda kneels down on one knee, allowing herself to get closer to Simon and paying even more attention to the tale. Fascinated by what she hears, once again she envisions the tale exactly as it had happened....

A horse's distressing neigh is heard well in the distance and an uncanny feeling comes over the farmer. The wild animal cries recklessly from within the thick haze, just beyond the farmer's view, on the horizon where the dark clouds had first appeared. The horse's call has a discernable sound of torment, which sends shivers right down the middle of the farmer's back.

The farmer strains his eyes, squinting to see, and gazes deep into the remoteness from where he heard the ghostly cry. His hair and clothing wave sporadically as the wind steadily increases. He grabs a tighter hold of his hat, and removes it from his head. Firmly he places it at his side to hold; the hat's brim rapidly beats against his thigh.

One can hear the steps of a hoofed animal thunder against the arid ground below, echoing louder as it approaches. All at once, the silhouette of a black horse and its rider appear through the intense fog, kicking up a trail of dust behind them. The farmer does not recognize the strange man who is quickly approaching. He stands there watching, waiting for a closer look. Details of the shadowy figure become more defined as he charges closer, racing toward the farmer from out of the dark mist.

The horse is a powerful beast, pitch black like the moonless night. His velvet coat shines a midnight-blue when the light hits it just right.

His large nostrils flare with great ferocity, with the horse's nerves and muscles twitching unsteadily as if ready to do battle. The stallion's thick flowing mane tremors in the breeze as it gallops ever closer, with its eyes glowing a fiery red.

The stallion's rider is even more menacing and frightful in appearance, if that were even possible. Uncommonly tall and large, the shadowy man has broad, massive shoulders that almost spread out to the width of his horse. His black, broad-brimmed hat makes the stranger appear to be more of a silhouette than an actual being. The shadow cast from the hat cleverly disguises any discernible features of the stranger's face, making him appear more dangerous, threatening, and mysterious. Like his steed, his eyes also glow a fiery red—reflecting an anger that dwells deep from within his blazing soul.

The rider charges his horse feverishly with his animal directly aimed toward the farmer, running at the stallion's top speed. As he approaches, the farmer notices an elongated golden staff that the stranger is holding in his hand. It appears to be some sort of symbol of authority or perhaps a sorcerer's weapon. At the top end of the staff rests a large sapphire-colored gemstone, shimmering in its setting, which is also encased by gold. The glow of the gemstone combined with the blaze burning within their fiery eyes contrast brightly against the darkened sky surrounding them. As the horse and its rider gallop fiendishly closer, the light cast from blue stone somewhat illuminates their way through the dark clouds and low-lying fog.

The sorcerer halts the horse to a running stop before the farmer. The stallion feverishly stands on his hind legs—a mixed show of courage, strength, and sheer panic. The farmer's wife, hearing the commotion, comes out of the cabin to see what is happening. She stands in the distance, holding their baby protectively in her arms, affectionately cradling him.

"Does someone dare to desecrate the sacred land of Gispan," the shadowy man cries out. "The burial place of my son?" he sounds aloud, pronouncing claim of ownership to the property. The dark stranger looks and points at the farmer, his fierce eyes looking deep within the farmer's soul.

Terrified by the mystical stranger, the farmer pleads with the dark outline of the man. "Sir, I didn't know it was your land," he exclaims; he is concerned for his own family's welfare much more so than his own. "I apologize; is there any way I can make it up to you?" The frightened farmer beseeches the evil sorcerer earnestly in fear, "You name it," he willingly offers.

Smoke flairs out of the stallion's nostrils, the horse behaving in a wild and unsteady way. He knows that something cursed and sinister is about to soon follow.

The evil sorcerer looks around; all is black now in the dark, misty fog. He looks to the farmer's house, trying to think of some form of payment for desecrating his son's sacred burial ground. In the distance he sees the farmer's wife and son standing there. She looks onward terrified, her baby crying incessantly. The farmer hears his troubled child in the distance and sees that the evil Gispan has also taken notice of them....

Interrupting Simon's story and unable to take any more suspense, Sigmund asks, "What happened next? Tell me, tell me!"

Simon retorts "You know you numbskull. You were there, remember?"

"Oh yeah," Sigmund replies, all caught up in the moment. "I forgot. Go on."

With fervor returning in his voice, Simon continues the tale. Everyone pictures the story as if it were happening all over again.

The mighty and evil Gispan has made a decision, one he believes befitting for desecrating his son's sacred burial place.

"You shall leave this place," he announces with a fiery blaze of red-hot anger stirred deep from within his soul. "And to be sure that there is nothing here for you," the sorcerer pauses for a moment looking around, immediately seeing the farmer's wife and child. Without hesitation, he conjures up one of his wicked spells. "There will be nothing for you here!" he shouts to the farmer. His horse neighs wildly and viciously.

In that very same instant, in a small fraction of the farmer's very own heartbeat, an intense ball of flame emerges from the sorcerer's evil staff. Like a bolt of lightning, the blue molten flame shoots out from the sacred sapphire stone at the end of his scepter, striking both the woman and child at the same time. Instantly it engulfs the two of them, transforming them into two oval stones, one larger, one smaller. Simultaneously both stones fall to the ground, firmly standing upright in place. The shadowy villain laughs evilly, the earth around him echoing with his maniacal laughter.

The humble farmer stands there helplessly. He sees the lifeless stones where his wife and child stood only moments ago. He hears the evil stranger still resounding with laughter, pleasantly amused by the farmer's loss. Regardless of consequence, the farmer is not about to give in without a fight.

The farmer immediately charges the sorcerer, catching the villain by surprise. Overcome and distraught with emotion, using all of his strength and might, he pulls the dark stranger off his horse. The farmer holds the wicked man down utilizing every ounce of force in his God-given body, shaking him against the ground as he pleads to him to return his family. His move is both brave and at the same time foolish. "Turn them back! Turn them back!" he shouts; he begs the heartless villain for mercy.

Gispan just laughs in return, unphased by the farmer's meek, mortal actions. "Only you can turn them back now," he tells him. "You, and a magical potion," he mysteriously tells the farmer.

The farmer does not know what to make of the statement. He does not realize it, but one day those exact words will continually resound in his mind, forever haunting him.

Suddenly the ground starts to shake with forcefulness, filled with the evil power of the villain. The sorcerer is still lying beneath the weight of the farmer as he desperately tries to hold him down. Sadly, the farmer's strength is of no merit. Gispan magically disappears into the ground, sinking as quicksand would into the earth, with his laugh fading as he vanishes into the ground beneath. His horse and staff both disappear with him—melting and vanishing somewhere deep below. For a moment, all becomes still and quiet.

The farmer remains lying there, motionless, positioned as if he were still holding the sorcerer against the immobile ground below him. Physically exhausted, he is breathing heavily, trying to regain his composure. He grabs a handful of soil, clenching it in his hands, and releases the grains like sand flowing through an hourglass. To him, the moments feel like hours as he watches the tiny pieces of dirt and ash fall right through his fingers.

"Where did he go?" he asks. "How can I get my family back?" The farmer is perplexed and disturbed by the inexplicable appearance and then disappearance of the shadowy man. The villain's wrath, however, is not over….

The ground into which the sorcerer vanished begins to shake once again. This time even more ferociously than before, if that is even possible. Once again the earth suddenly becomes alive, the ground uprooting all around the powerless farmer. All kinds of black, sinister-looking plants begin to sprout and grow all around, plants that quickly turn to shrubs, shrubs that turn to trees, trees that turn into a forest. The newly born forest is lifeless, dark, and dismal.

Simon pauses and slowly Amiranda begins to hear Simon's words again, as her imagination of the tale slowly dissipates. This time her attention stays focused on the storyteller and not the tale.

Simon continues, now concluding his story. "Massive portions of the ground were displaced by the evil Gispan's mighty powers. The once fertile meadow was, in an instant, overcome with lifeless vegetation, turning it into the Deciduous Forest as we now know it. Today, only the farmer's house remains, overrun with trees, weeds, and shrubs."

Simon takes a deep breath, his emotional telling of the tale clearly affecting him.

"Just the house," he repeats himself. "The house and two stones that mysteriously lie in wait out front."

The group remains still, silent in disbelief of Simon's incredible yet truthful story. In the past, Amiranda has imagined and heard many strange and wonderful tales of the forest, but none before were quite like this. People often try to explain the inexplicable, and in so doing, come up with as many far-fetched stories as there are stars in the sky. This one was by far the strangest and most unbelievable story that she had ever heard.

Still, something in her heart tells her it is true. It is as if she has always known, or had dreamed about it, but never quite recalled it—that is, until now. The simple fact of it all is why wouldn't she believe it? After all, she was hearing it from a two-headed talking turtle.

Allowing a moment for his story to sink in, Simon pauses once again. He tries to regain his original thought.

"I hear the man now stays alone in the house that was built on the forbidden territory, trying to make this magical potion the sorcerer was speaking of. No one else dares come into the forest, as everyone is deathly afraid of the evil sorcerer." Simon's tone of voice eases. "Speaking of which," he adds lightheartedly, "what is a young girl like you doing in the woods all alone?"

At first, Amiranda is captivated by the exciting and emotional impact of the tale. The many questions she had all these years about the forest were somehow put into a different light, if Simon's story were indeed true. Still, to her, many more questions remain.

Amiranda suddenly remembers the task at hand. "My nanny is very sick," she explains; "we've come to seek a cure." The young princess stands up, picking up her pup, Peatie, for every time she mentions her sick Nana she seeks some sort of comfort. She continues, "They say that the only one who can help us is a man they call the Savant who supposedly lives in these woods." She then recalls the farmer in Simon's story. "Is he the man about whom you were speaking?"

Simon thinks to himself for a moment, and then turns his head toward his companion Sigmund. "Ah I see," he says, "but what they say is only partially true."

"What do you mean?" Amiranda asks. She is clearly worried about her Nana.

"We can help you too, can't we Sigmund?" he says enthusiastically, volunteering and offering both their services. Peatie barks with enthusiasm.

"Yeah," Sigmund replies, agreeing with Simon before realizing exactly what he agreed to. "What? Wait a minute!" he finally objects.

"Sure!" Simon confirms, speaking not only for himself, but also for his not-so-willing partner. "We can help you find this man. We haven't been on an adventure in years. It'll be fun!" The kind turtle is more than eager to help Amiranda, and genuinely so.

Sigmund, on the other hand, is only concerned with his own well-being. For him, he would rather be left excluded from any risky and unnecessary undertakings.

"I dunno. It sounds kind of dangerous;" he expresses his reluctance. "He's all the way on the other side of the woods—and besides, I haven't had my dinner yet." The hesitant turtle is used to making up excuses, no matter how absurd they may seem.

"You know where to find him?" Amiranda exclaims excitedly. Full of hope, her crystal-blue eyes light up and sparkle even more than usual.

"Sure!" Simon concurs, much in the same manner as before. Sigmund makes a throat clearing "Ahem."

"Uh well, not exactly," Simon corrects himself, "but we can help you find him!" The kind turtle sounds quite confident that they can help her.

"I have a feeling I'm going to regret this," Sigmund complainingly pouts.

With a reawakened bounce in her step, Amiranda exclaims, "It's all set then!" She hugs Peatie tightly, happy that there is a sign of hope to her mission.

With everything set, Amiranda, Peatie, Reynolds, Sigmund, and

Simon all set out together on their journey deeper into the forest.

The group starts walking farther into the woods along the long and winding trail. The path begins to narrow, becoming less and less traveled the deeper into the woods the travelers get. Reynolds flies along in pace with the entourage, careful not to lead too far or fall too far behind. Although both Sigmund and Simon are turtles sharing one shell, they maintain a surprisingly good pace with Amiranda and her friends. Although they fall a bit behind, it is not as much as Amiranda had originally imagined they would.

"You guys walk pretty fast for a turtle," Amiranda points out quite surprised.

Simon laughs, "That's because we're racing turtles."

"Things sure are different here from what I'm used to," Amiranda remarks, looking around every which way in the dark moonlit forest. She wonders what other strange encounters will come to pass. "Well, at least this is a change of pace." The princess quickly realizes her play on words and giggles. "Didn't mean it like that," she apologizes.

Sigmund finds an opportunistic moment to be sarcastic once again. "Great, turtle jokes. Everyone loves turtle jokes," he murmurs.

"Oh it's quite alright," Simon tells her, just happy to have her company. For him, it is a change of pace as well. It is quite nice to have someone else to chat with—someone more personable than his unruly sibling Sigmund, who is always breathing down the back of his neck—many times, quite literally.

The group reaches a small, well-lit clearing, lit only by some moonlight shining through a small opening in the canopy of tree branches above.

"It's getting late," Amiranda says, stating the obvious and judging the lack of light by which to travel. "We should probably settle down for the night—right guys?"

Sigmund was just waiting for those words to be uttered. "I thought you'd never ask."

Amiranda opens her pillowcase. She pulls out a small quilt handmade by her Nana and opens it up. She spreads out the blanket on top of some leaves to help cushion them, so they all lie down to try to get a good night's rest. Peatie helps by stretching the blanket. He bites on one of the corners and pulls it taught, firmly tugging it into position.

The princess sits herself upright on the blanket and her young pup circles around before finding a comfortable place to rest. As usual, he lies right beside Amiranda's feet for comfort. Reynolds plops himself down on the blanket, tired from flying the whole trip. Being an indoor parrot, he is not accustomed to flying for so long. Sigmund and Simon also settle themselves nearby, ready to eat and rest.

Amiranda pulls some snacks for dinner out from her pouch and shares them with her animal friends. She has sunflower seeds for Reynolds and breaks off pieces of her sandwich to give to Peatie. She kindly pulls some lettuce from the sandwich and shares it with the two turtles.

Comforted by one another's company, the princess and her friends all rest as they try to regain their strength for the next day. The group's camaraderie partially negates any uneasy or frightening feelings made by the night, the group now all alone in the dark, mysterious woods. This will be the first time Amiranda has ever slept away from home, not safely tucked in her own comfy bed. Quietly they all settle in, eating and finishing their meals.

Just before they all go to sleep, Simon bravely tries to comfort

Amiranda. “I’ll keep first watch,” he offers heroically, “so you need not worry about anything.” The kind turtle lifts his head proudly, as if seeking praise. “And I’m sure Sigmund will take over for me—won’t you Sigmund?”

“Sure.” Once again, Sigmund answers before realizing what he has agreed to. “What? I’ll be in my shell.” The selfish turtle retracts his head into his armor-plated shell, a perfect place for protection from the unknown.

Simon retorts back at him, “You’ll be on watch is what you will be.” He then turns to the princess. “Don’t worry Amiranda,” he reassures her, “We will have everything covered.”

Gladly, Simon takes charge of the situation. He is obviously doing his best to try to impress her. Amiranda smiles back graciously at him as she lies down to rest for the night. Snugly she wraps part of her quilt around her and her pup. She holds him close to her just like a child would hold their favorite doll or stuffed teddy bear in bed. Reynolds perches himself nearby, on a low-lying branch just adjacent to Amiranda, careful as always not to be too far away from the rest of the group.

Quietly and kindly they all say good night as they finally settle down to try and get some rest. Little do they know that their journey has only just begun. Even if they do make it through the night, tomorrow they have a long trek ahead of them.

Simon takes the first watch as promised.

Chapter 11

Daylight

Morning has come and all are still fast asleep—even Simon and Sigmund; who were *supposed* to keep watch. The woods do not look nearly as scary now as they appeared to be late last night. Surprisingly, there are some birds that are heard singing in the distance as the sun is shining brightly through the tree branches. At this time of day, the angle of the sun's light allows it to pass and enter just beneath the layer of clouds that constantly hover over the forest. The air tastes sweet and a cool, calm breeze blows; the leaves softly rustle. Nevertheless, deep within the

Deciduous Forest, the trees around them are mostly all bare. The leaves on the ground are all dried, lifeless and brown, not the way an ordinary spring day should be.

Little by little, as the sun slowly rises, a beam of light gradually makes its way across the tree branches, and finally illuminates the group through a small clearing in the trees. Like a beacon, the beam of light shines down directly over Amiranda's eyes, gently waking her. Slowly the princess opens one eye, looking around her while still remaining motionless.

Instinctually, Peatie wakes up at the same time she does. Like he does each and every morning, ritualistically he licks the tip of her nose, showing his affection toward the princess. He wags his tail frantically and then jumps around anxiously, ready to start the morning.

Amiranda, however, is still taking her time in waking up. She hugs him good morning, sits up, and then stretches her arms outward toward the sun. Finally she takes in a deep breath of the fresh morning air, allowing it to fill her lungs. Hopefully it will help give her the energy she needs to face the day. After all, it has been a long night, as the young princess is not used to sleeping outdoors.

Amiranda glances over at the turtles who are still quietly resting in their shells. With the tip of her finger, she softly taps the top of their shell to wake them.

"Hey, I thought you guys were going to keep watch. We all should be wide awake by now. We've got a big day ahead," she reminds them, more than anxious to continue on with her quest. She has not changed her mind since last night, even considering all the tales told about evil sorcerers and enchanted forests coming from talking animals. Perhaps she *was* dreaming....

Simon pops his head out of his shell. "Uh, what?" he yawns, just waking up. With his eyes still squinting from the sunlight, he takes a moment to allow them to adjust to the light. "Sigmund, wake up!" he tells him; "I told you to keep watch hours ago."

Still mostly asleep, Sigmund replies. "Five more minutes, please," his mumbling voice echoes within his shell.

Hearing all the commotion, Reynolds finally wakes up. The parrot stretches his wings before perching himself on Amiranda's shoulder.

"Wake up. Arrk! Wake up!" he echoes loudly. "Big day. Warrk! Big day!" he repeats Amiranda's words, overhearing them while still half-asleep.

Even though Reynolds appears anxious, you can tell that he did not get much rest himself last night, as he is not used to sleeping outdoors, let alone in some dark, mysterious forest. Nevertheless, the smell of the fresh outdoors and the chance to finally fly free outside reinvigorates the parrot, and he is quickly ready to continue onward with their journey. Unfortunately, the same does not hold true for some of the other animals....

Sigmund, the last one to wake up, reluctantly pops his head out from his shell. Just as soon as the turtle does, an acorn falls right on top of it. *Clunk!*

"I knew I was going to regret this," he says grumbling. Another one quickly follows. *Thump!*

Amiranda and her friends all laugh as they look up to the tree branches above them, curious to see the cause of the commotion. Apparently, a gray squirrel is intentionally dropping the acorns directly onto Sigmund's head. With great accuracy, he drops the missiles with military precision one by one onto his target.

"Ah gotcha Sigmund!" the heckling squirrel chuckles and laughs jokingly.

"Just what I needed," Sigmund declares, reaffirming that fact that he *should* have stayed in his shell today.

Simon smiles back and shouts out to the squirrel, "Hey, Sherman, good pal! Nice to see you!"

Evidently, the playful squirrel is a former acquaintance of the twin turtles. While Simon and Sherman clearly have a history of a past camaraderie with one another, Sigmund, on the other hand, has become more of a target for Sherman's practical jokes—quite literally. It is ironic how the two turtles take on two very different attitudes toward the gray squirrel, just as they do toward life itself.

Hearing the animals talking again, Amiranda finally convinces herself that she was not dreaming last night. She stands up straight, her head looking high up into the trees. Trying to block the bright morning sun, she places her hand over her eyes, squinting for a better look.

"My, you two know one another?" Amiranda asks Simon, still unable to obtain a good visual.

Peatie is also unsure of what to make of the furry-tailed squirrel. He yelps at the acorn-throwing stranger, ever protective of Amiranda. Reynolds flies to a nearby branch, staying clear of the squirrel's projectile-throwing range while still being able to maintain a watchful eye on him. For the first time, the house-trained parrot almost makes a perfect landing, basically getting the hang of flying around outside. All the practice seems to be improving his self-learned flying skills. All eyes follow Sherman as he climbs down from the trees, scurrying skillfully like the master climber he is.

"Yeah," Simon casually replies to Amiranda's question; "Sherman and I go way back. We've been through some tough times too—ain't that right, Sherm?" Simon abbreviates his friend's name like good ol' friends often do. The squirrel finally makes it to the group, scampering onto the blanket just beside them.

"Sure have, but what are you doing over this way?" Sherman asks inquisitively. "This is quite far from where you usually hang around—especially with Sigmund never wanting to go anywhere."

"We're helping our friends here, they're seeking the man who lives in these woods," Simon explains, speaking for the whole group. Clearly, he has proudly accepted Amiranda's mission. "She needs to find a cure for her Nana."

In just about the blink of an eye, Sherman's eyes light up, as he loves the idea of serving on any type of duty or assignment. You can almost visualize the wheels in his mind churning, concentrating with such military prowess, as he construes some sort of objective and a means toward a goal. In this case, the mission is to find the Savant.

"Well why didn't you say so?" he asks, more than ready to lend a hand, or in this case, a paw. "I can help. I know where to find him," he asserts.

Sherman thinks to himself for a moment while he gently rubs the fur on the tip of his chin, as if deep in thought. He begins to calculate the best way to get there while considering obstacles they might encounter. A red flag goes up in his mind and the group sees the concern expressed in his eyes.

"But it can get kind of dangerous," he continues to warn them, himself unafraid of the many risks that lie ahead.

Sigmund states the obvious, "I knew I should have stayed in bed."

He pops his head back into his shell. Obviously, he wants to be no part of this plan.

With a rekindled spark of hope gleaming in her eyes, Amiranda exclaims, "Oh, thank you guys! I don't know what I would ever do without you."

Amiranda begins to curtsy but stops herself just before doing so, careful once again not to reveal her royal upbringing. She quickly releases the pleats of her dress.

"Pleased to meet you Sherman," she bows her head, "this is Peatie and this is Reynolds." The princess motions to her two companions, introducing both of them with the simple sway of her arm. Peatie yelps a friendly and warm "hello." No longer feeling apprehensive, Reynolds finally flies back to perch on Amiranda's shoulder, his landings getting better and better the more he flies. They are all introduced to one another, smiling cordially.

Amiranda is eager to get started. She readies herself by ironing any wrinkles in her dress with the stroke of her hands, dusting herself off and brushing out the creases at the same time. She interlocks her fingers as she carefully stretches her arms, extending them way up high over her head for one last good stretch. Reynolds spreads his wings much in the same manner, high up above him, echoing her exact motion. Knowing that there will be an arduous journey ahead of them, Amiranda takes another deep breath and stretches, while Reynolds does the same, mimicking her not only with words, but with actions.

"Come on guys. We've got some work to do," Amiranda confidently declares. She then begins to prepare her things for the day's expedition.

The princess grabs her gear, packing what is left, carefully into her pillowcase. She then ties it once again, binding it into a knot and attaches it to one end of her broomstick. Placing it over her shoulder, she steadies it, ready to move on.

Although the group has only just met, Amiranda has great confidence in her new friends as they have great faith in her as well. Instantly, the camaraderie and teamwork of the crew binds the group together and pushes them onward. With everyone working together, it seems as if the group can accomplish almost anything.

All walk deeper into the woods, this time with Sherman leading the way.

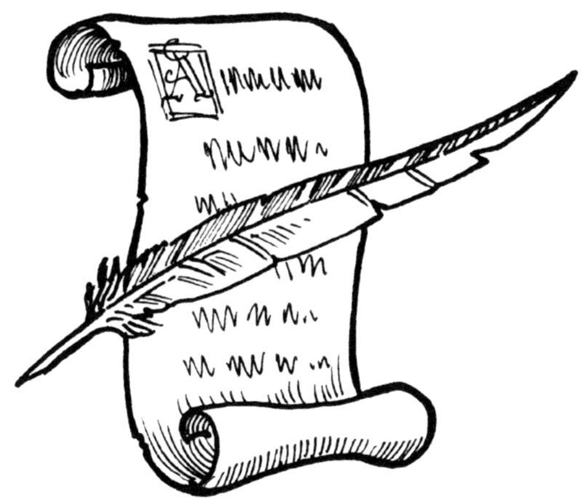

Chapter 12

The Note

Meanwhile, back at the castle, for the moment all is quiet. Jove hurriedly enters the room, ready and anxious to face another day. "Amiranda, hurry down here!" the proficient butler calls out to her, the way he does each and every morning. "Once again you are behind schedule. Are you oversleeping again?"

He prepares the sheet music on the piano and gets everything ready for the princess, but still there is not a peep coming from upstairs. There are absolutely no signs or sound of Amiranda or her pup Peatie.

"Hurry up, Amiranda, we haven't got all day," he hastily yells out to her. Still, there is no reply as Amiranda does not answer. It is just then that Jove notices something peculiar—Reynold's cage is empty and the brass cage door is flung wide open. Jove begins to look around, wondering where the parrot is.

"That pesky bird must have gotten out once again," Jove says to himself. He looks all around the room, trying to see where Reynolds may be hiding. The great window is closed so he realizes that the parrot could not have gone too far. Jove then calls up once again as he makes his way across the checkerboard floor and up the marble staircase to Amiranda's bedroom.

"I have no time for games, Amiranda, you mustn't keep me waiting. It is time to wake up!" the butler yells out loud as he ascends the stairs.

Jove gets to Amiranda's door, opens it up, and sees no sign of the princess or her two pets. For the first time in his career, he does not know where the princess is. Suddenly, he sees a note left on the dresser.

The butler knows that Amiranda keeps everything in precise order and arranged just so—after all, he helped raise her to be that way. Picking up the paper, he quietly reads it to himself. About two sentences into reading it, he realizes that Amiranda is gone.

Frantically he drops the note back on the dresser and quickly heads out of the room.

"Your majesty! Your majesty!" he cries out loud as he exits.

Seconds later, Jove waits just outside the doorway as the king and queen enter Amiranda's room.

"It is right over there, on the dresser," Jove explains, his voice shaky and filled with fear. He cannot bear to reenter the room, wanting to leave everything just as it is.

King Jedrek picks up the letter. His wife, Queen Isabel, stands at his side. The two are befuddled by the whole situation. Reading it together, it says:

Dear Mom and Dad,

I am sorry that I have left, but I promise I will be back, God willing. I have taken both Peatie and Reynolds into the forest. I know I should not listen in on your royal conversations, but when Roxen came, I could not help myself to see what he was up to. After he left, I overheard the doctor tell of Nana's ailment, as there was no way for me to leave without being caught.

We will go out and find the Savant—as it is our only hope of saving Nana. I hope you understand. Please forgive me.

Your loving daughter,
Amiranda.

Reading the note several times over, the king and queen look at one another, as they hold each other tighter. For the first time in years, the two can be seen together, in the same place and at the same time.

They knew this day would someday come—the day their daughter would have to face the world out on her own—but no matter how much they prepared her for that day, they never really prepared themselves. They look out the very same window that Amiranda has gazed out of a million times over. For the first time, they see things the way she sees them to be.

Chapter 13

The River

The group travels even farther along the trail, all following Sherman's lead. After hours of hiking, it is about midday when they finally reach a wide river obstructing their path. The river flows steadily downstream, somewhat in the direction they need to travel. Both sides of the riverbank are bordered by a thick dense row of the forest's trees. For them to safely swim across would be most precarious and outright dangerous, due to the swift current and the sharp-edged rocks resting just above and hiding just below the water level.

Surprisingly, unlike the rest of the lifeless and ill-fated forest, the river's edge is the one place in the forest where the leaves and the trees are growing green and fertile, as they are continually nurtured by the river's life-giving waters. The sun glistens radiantly off the waves of the river, shining like rays of hope in the midst of the deep, dark forest.

"What do we do now?" Amiranda asks, trying to think of another way across.

Once again, Sigmund finds another opportunity to complain. "Nice going, Sherman," he says cynically to the furry leader.

The squirrely leader pays him no mind as he is more than prepared to handle the situation. Sherman is well aware of the slight obstacle they would encounter. "Simple" he offers, rest-assuredly. "We'll just climb up the trees and leap from one branch to the next until we make our way across to the other side."

The heroic squirrel lifts his head high, tall and proud of his own expertise. The height of the trees is quite small in comparison to someone of his high ability. Certainly if someone his size can overcome such an obstacle, surely they must be able to do so as well.

Sherman smirks, standing there patiently waiting for everyone else to join in with his joyfulness. However, much to his surprise, this is not the case. There seems to be the look of confusion seen in the other traveler's faces as they look at him, and then look at one another, and then finally back at him. Sherman's smile quickly fades.

"That may be fine for you, but what about the rest of us?" Simon finally exclaims.

"Oh," Sherman pauses, taking a minute to realize what should have been so obvious to him. He pardons himself, "I didn't think of that. It has always worked for me before." Sherman has been taken aback now that his well-contrived plan has been totally knocked of course by this small minor detail.

"Anyone else got any bright ideas?" Sigmund groans sarcastically. As dim-witted as he seems, even Sigmund knows their limitations.

The group remains standing at water's edge, looking downward to the swift flowing current rushing right by their feet, then outward to the river running rapidly all the way to the other side. There is nowhere safe for everyone to cross.

Amiranda coaxes the group on. "Come on guys, we have to think of a way." The sound of the rushing water surges beside them as they all try to think.

Sherman offers up another plan. "I got it!" the squirrel says, with that same authoritative tone as before; although, this time he is a bit more convincing. "I remember seeing a wooden raft just down a bit," he tells them. "We can take it along the river, which will bring us close to where we're going."

Watching the turbulent waters before them, the group sees no other reasonable alternative. Somewhat reluctantly, once again they all follow Sherman's command; hopefully this time it will pay off.

They all walk along the edge of the riverbank, following the trail that travels alongside the steady stream. Little by little, the waters become calmer as the river gradually widens. From all the walking they grow more and more tired, and even somewhat restless. Finally, they come to a man-made raft resting near the riverbank. The makeshift raft is literally a bunch of small twigs and branches tied together with some twisted, tattered, and torn looking vines.

"Are all of us are supposed to ride on *that*?" Sigmund asks, being not too optimistic in the answer.

Simon turns his head to look at his counterpart, Sigmund, finding that there is just no escaping him. Whimsically he retorts, "Oh, who asked you to come along? Where's your sense of adventure?"

Sigmund quickly silences.

Although not nearly seaworthy, Amiranda looks over the crude raft, hesitates for one moment and then offers her approval of the weary vessel. "Well, it's all we got," she tells them quite simply.

The princess pushes the raft into the water and to everyone's amazement it floats. Holding the raft steady, she grabs a long and lanky stick with which she will push and guide the raft.

Before totally committing herself, she carefully tests out the raft by slowly putting some of her weight on it, climbing aboard one small step at a time. She is cautious not to make any sudden movements. Surprisingly, the raft holds without too much of a problem, with the top of the raft resting just above the water level.

She gives it her final blessing "It's okay guys, climb aboard!" Amiranda doesn't let on to her own skepticism. She is anxiously determined to continue on with her journey.

All make their way aboard the raft except for Reynolds who chooses to fly overhead. Considering the rickety condition of the raft, it is probably a much wiser and far safer choice. Amiranda directs the vessel by gently pushing her stick along the river's bottom as the current carries the raft and all those aboard steadily downstream. The group travels and drifts for a while until the river widens into a large, calm lake. It becomes by far, the most peaceful and relaxing part of their journey.

The drifters float effortlessly aboard the raft, taking a much-needed rest from their long trek. Comfortably, they all soak in the midday sun. Even Reynolds has chosen to take a break from flying and perches himself on top of the raft, finally trusting it somewhat. Eventually they come to the middle of the lake where there is absolutely no current pushing or pulling on the vessel—and all becomes perfectly calm, still, and quiet.

Looking from above, the raft is their own small and isolated island, resting there motionless—square center in the tranquil lake, keeping them at a safe distance from the mysterious forest, which surrounds the area around them. There is a clearing in the clouds above, which allows the sun to shine right on through.

Amiranda lies there on her back, looking up at the sky while all the time cradling her pup as he sleeps. The princess sighs, her mind dreaming about her life back home, her pet goldfish, Molly, her Nana, and of things yet to come.

For the first time, the voyagers get a chance to enjoy the wondrous surroundings of nature's sheer beauty without worrying. The sounds of the lake both calm and soothe them as they listen to the gentle splish-splash of the waters around them. In the near distance they hear the mellow chirps made by birds—birds singing songs of love, of hope, and of peace. They can also hear the faint sounds of other timid noises made by some small woodland critters living near the water bank, as for here they are clear of the dark and unforgiving forest, at least for the time being.

Amiranda and her friends are all are perfectly quiet as they rest; the sun's light radiantly massaging their inner souls. After a while of resting, Amiranda sits up and gazes deep down into the waters. It is almost as if she were searching or looking for something. Peatie remains there fast asleep, still tired from their journey. He is not used to such long hikes, especially being as small as he is. The princess remains diligently staring into the water below, and looking at her own likeness flickering in the water as it is softly reflected.

Simon finally breaks the silence by beginning to tell another one of his tales.

"You know they call this the *'River of Reflection,'*" he states proudly; offering up the information as a bit of trivial knowledge. This is unlike the mysterious story told late last night, which seemed more like a fairy tale than an actual occurrence. "It is said that whoever looks deeply into it can see shades of the past and predictions about the future."

"You really don't believe in that stuff, do you?" remarks Sigmund. His voice is both skeptical and cowardly at the same time, clearly nervous about anything not of the ordinary.

Amiranda peers deeper and deeper into the translucent mystic-blue waters below—the same deep-blue color that closely matches her eyes.

"Really?" she asks curiously. There is an indication of disbelief in her reply. Just as equally, there is a hint of optimism in her voice; the princess only wishing to see into her own future. Initially nothing happens.

Earnestly, Amiranda continues to stare, hoping … wanting … wishing … waiting. Regretfully, she sees only her own reflection in the water, herself gazing down upon the glassy waters, which are almost mirrorlike in their image. The only exception is the small rippling of the gentle waves in the water, which partially distorts her face, somewhat twisting her figure as well. Looking at herself, everything remains unchanged, and nothing appears to be different.

As her reflection shimmers, her own likeness slowly mesmerizes her. The sounds of the lake and the wildlife surrounding them cause the princess to gently go into a trance. Slowly, those sounds echo louder and louder in her mind. Then, just as quickly they all dissipate—gradually becoming much more muffled and faint. Steadily, the sounds disappear completely, remaining far distant from the thoughts that are deeply embedded in her mind.

Suddenly without warning, her image is transformed in the water, just as she had wished and hoped that it would. Amiranda begins to see images of people and events in her life—all in no particular sequence or order. It is like a crystal ball that has gone haywire, showing her random visions of the past, present, and possible future. The princess now has no choice but to watch intensely as the images unravel before her.

First, she envisions her parents worrying about her, her father consoling her mother, both of them reading the note that she left for them on the dresser. The two look out the window to the pond, then to the field below and finally to the forest in the distance. Amiranda is nowhere to be found. The princess quickly realizes that it is the present that she sees.

Next, she sees herself much younger, as a child, playing in the field on a particularly warm spring day. Amiranda remembers when she used to carry on like any normal child would, with her Nana vigilantly watching over her from that same second story window of her bedroom. Although she never had the best kind of an upbringing, she still relishes her childhood and memories of her nanny. That image is quickly transformed—to something much darker and much graver.

She pictures an image of her goldfish, Molly, in the waters where she had just left her. Molly is unmistakably frightened, surrounded by other larger fish circling around her, viewing and sizing her up at every possible angle. Viciously they swim around her like sharks circling around their prey before they dine. What a small feast it would be too, as Molly is dwarfed in size compared to the much larger fish surrounding her.

The tiny black goldfish darts around a maze of seaweed and hides in the crevices of some small rocks—narrowly escaping the jaws of the larger fish's mouths and razor sharp teeth as they try to grab hold of her. Breathing a sigh of relief, Molly remains there in the dark, uncertain of what other dangers may lie ahead.

The image transforms again, this time she sees her Nana much younger, tucking the young princess into bed when she was very little. Amiranda vaguely remembers those days of her childhood, when life was much simpler and the most she had to worry about was which doll she was going to play with next or what dress up outfit she was going to wear. She recalls how she loved to play "princess" way back when. Oh how she yearns for those days. How simple and joyous they were.

Then unexpectedly, her vision is blackened and violently transformed to where she sees her nanny severely ill in bed, doing worse than when Amiranda last saw her. Nana is lying there resting, with her doctor standing right beside her. He watches her, looking on hopelessly. Clearly, there is nothing he can do to help her. The princess is uncertain if it is the present or future that she sees. Amiranda is more concerned than ever; in fact she is outright scared that her nanny's condition may be worsening.

Soon thereafter, visions of the Deciduous Forest make their way into her trance, along with many of the perils she will eventually face. Somewhere in the back of her mind she sees bits and pieces of different images.

First, she witnesses some giant, dark green, and pitch black "spiderlike" crabs. Although not totally vivid and clear, the vicious crabs seem to be grasping at the group with their huge claws. Loud, snapping sounds are heard coming from their razor-sharp pinchers. Menacingly, they try to take hold of her and her animal friends.

That image quickly fades and she next sees herself falling down a waterfall in a raft, falling helplessly into nowhere, drowning in the mist of the waters below. All of the images are quick, abrupt, and un-telling. They are like a dream that constantly changes from one event to the next, leaving far more questions than answers.

Lastly, she envisions an intense fire, which quickly engulfs the forest and everything around—consuming all in its path. Deep from within the flame, she sees a pair of fiery-red eyes that glow ominously. She knows undoubtedly that they must belong to the mighty and evil villain Gispan, the wicked sorcerer of the forest.

Just as suddenly as they all came, all of the images rapidly fade, dissipating into nothingness—a mere memory, if that. Amiranda is left staring into her own eyes and looking at her own face, as her image flickers ever so gently in the delicate waves of the rippling water. She ponders over the river's transfiguration and as to what to make of its prophecy. Her emotions become a mixture of every feeling she has ever lived and ever realized.

The fluttering she feels in her heart and the pit felt deep in her stomach also put the princess further at unease. She fears that in making her choice to come into the forest, her intrusion might somehow change the future—perhaps irrevocably for the worse. Her Nana, her parents, her new woodland friends, even the whole town of Luxing could be at risk. Each one affected by her reckless voyage into the forest, a place she was told not to have entered right from the start.

Amiranda gazes at her reflection, watching it as it slowly returns,

thinking of all the visions she saw. A million and one thoughts circle around in her mind, instantly filling every nook and cranny of the space, leaving her no room to process any of them. Taken aback by the images, she vacantly stares into the water for what seems like hours even though only seconds pass. Just then, interrupting her own thoughts, something immediately pops its head out of the water.

The princess gasps, startled by the surprise.

"Hey guys! I saw you all from below!" A rather puffy, large round fish says with much friendliness. He is a large, yellow blowfish and clearly an old kind acquaintance to the other animals the princess had just met.

"Hey, Gordy!" Sherman exclaims joyfully. "Where are your other friends—the blowfish gang?"

Three other blowfish emerge just behind their leader, popping their heads out one by one in a triangular fashion. All of Gordy's entourage resembles their leader, except they all are different sizes and have different physical features. Gordy himself is the most fit in both size and shape, he being the leader of them all.

The three blowfish all chime in, each one giving their own personal greeting.

"Hey gang!" the slender one says, waving his fin. "I'm Riley." Riley's voice is much higher in pitch than the other blowfish due to his scrawny size.

"What's going on? I'm Stiley" announces the one directly next to him, his voice slightly deeper due to his average size. Stiley has a certain amount of class and coolness in his demeanor when he speaks, being the laid-back type that he is. He also appears calm and collected at all times, not letting anything or anyone faze him.

"How's it going?" the last blowfish says in a baritone, being the heaviest and largest of the group. "I'm Trent, pleased to meet you." Amiranda and her friends all graciously smile and wave.

"What are you guys doing all the way out here?" Gordy asks inquisitively. "The water is certainly no place for you land idiots. By the way, nice raft," he remarks jokingly. While the raft may not be a sight for sore eyes, still, it remains afloat.

"We're helping our friend Amiranda here," Sherman replies, once again making himself the spokesperson for the crew. Amiranda gives a slight curtsy, pointing herself out in the group. She remains careful not to be too formal although she had always been taught differently. Still, some habits are hard to break.

Sherman continues, "She needs to find the man who lives in these woods. He is the only one who can help save her Nana who is very sick."

In an instant, in fact in less than a blink of an eye, Gordy's expression becomes far less casual and much more serious. "Oh, *family*. Now that's important," he tells her, showing himself to also follow that one simple golden rule. You can tell that Gordy is also close to his loved ones at home.

He stops and thinks to himself for a moment, centering his attention to the task at hand. Finally, he looks to Amiranda, telling her, "Well, you're going to need some help if you're going to face those mean ol' spider crabs along the way." The blowfish's ring leader is happy to help the princess with her mission.

Amiranda is stunned by the accuracy of his statement, clearly worried by what she saw just moments earlier in the reflection of the mystical waters. "Spider crabs?" she repeats nervously, almost stuttering.

"Yeah, mean suckers," Gordy confirms, with much inflection heard in the tone of his voice. "They'll claw you to shreds, tear ya to pieces, slice ya from limb to—" The blowfish leader stops himself midsentence, afraid to frighten the princess any more than he already has, seeing the worried expression on her face. "Ah, but no worries," he reassures her; "we'll take care of them for you. Am I right gang?"

The blowfish gang all responds eagerly in agreement, each one giving his own affirmative response.

"We'll shred 'em," Stiley says, much in the same calm, cool, and collected manner as before.

"Mortify 'em," Riley the slender one squeaks, punching his fins together repeatedly, ready for action.

"Eat 'em up and spit 'em out," Trent baritones, his teeth grinning widely.

Clearly, the blowfish clan all show no fear, being the brave, bold group that they are. They cannot wait to get their fins on those pesky, evil spider crabs.

With all in agreement to help on Amiranda's mission, Gordy then calls for additional backup.

"Hold on, let me get my reinforcements," he kindly tells them, wanting to gain some more strength in numbers, just to be safe and sure.

Gordy begins to take in a deep breath of air, which makes him puff out to nearly three times his original size, inflating himself into a large balloon-shaped fish. Pointy spikes protrude out every which way from his body—making him transition from being cute and cuddly to a rather strong, and even somewhat dangerous entity.

Forcefully, he then releases the air, which creates a loud whistle for all around to hear. "Hey gang! Hey Shiro!" he then yells out emphatically as he slowly returns to his original size.

Almost immediately, and in one great big giant wave, an enormous mass of blowfish all surface together. They are all of different shapes, different sizes, and some are even different colors. Each one obviously belonging to the same community from which Gordy and his main gang of friends reside. The large entourage of fish starts clamoring amongst themselves, wondering what caused all the sudden commotion.

There is much camaraderie amongst the group and they all appear happy to see one another, like one great big family reunion. Amiranda is overly impressed with the overwhelming outpouring of support. She smiles and welcomes them, looking every which way, not knowing who to acknowledge or say "hi" to first. They all greet her welcomingly.

As the chatter starts to settle down, a brightly colored Japanese samurai fish emerges from the deep waters right next to Gordy. Having traveled a greater distance than the blowfish, a whole army of Japanese fighting fish also emerges right behind their fearless samurai leader. Literally hundreds upon hundreds of them appear, all of whom are both eager and ready to fight.

Shiro, the leader of the vast Japanese fighting fish army, is by far the most colorful and majestic of the entire group. He has long, rainbow-colored fins that wave and flow in the water. They make him appear even more spectacular than any of the other samurai fish. He uses his fins like swords, slicing through the water effortlessly. Like a true master of karate, he also uses them to defend himself whenever necessary.

Shiro's eyes are predominantly slanted, but this more so has to do with him having bad eyesight than with being of Asian descent. He has to squint his eyes in order to see things around him; but this, by no means, detracts from his superior fighting skills, as he is a premier martial artist. His unassuming nature is his greatest advantage, for those who underestimate his skills as a samurai surely pay the price in doing so. After all, he uses all of his senses and talents combined—as he is not dependent on any one more so than the other. In short, Shiro is a true master of the martial arts, a warrior who maintains the highest honor, and a spiritual leader for all of his followers.

"Aye," Shiro says, putting great length in his response; "you called for Samurais?" He gestures his fin toward his group, referring to the name of his army. Whenever Shiro speaks, he talks using broken English, leaving out bits and pieces of proper grammar and sentence structure. Still, everyone can understand what he is saying. Shiro respectfully bows to Amiranda and her friends in the traditional Japanese style.

Gordy grins; he is pleased by the response of the group and the help of their grand master and sensei. "Yeah, we're going to make shells out of those mean spider crabs for my friends here," he tells him, motioning to Amiranda and her friends. "But to do so, we gotta go after their ringleader, 'Claws,'—you up to it?"

"Aye," Shiro replies again affirmatively, again taking his time to say such a small word. "Claws won't know what hit by," the samurai leader says using broken English as he faithfully bows his head once again. His whole army bows their heads behind him, all loyal to the cause and their noble leader.

The stage is now set. The greatest river battle of all time is about to take place—the battle between the blowfish and the Japanese fighting fish teamed up together, against the vicious spider crabs who control the river farther downstream. This is a tale that would never be believed, except by those who were there to witness it firsthand.

Chapter 14

A Man Amongst Men

Returning to the Magistrate's room, the king is standing before a few rows of about fifty men. Each one of the men is far unlike the next beside him, as some are skinnier and others huskier, some are shorter and others lankier, some clean shaven and others bearded. Still, all of these men are considered to be the bravest and most elite in the entire kingdom. Yule is at the doorway, standing firmly at attention as always. The king paces back and forth before the men, looking each one of them over before talking. He begins to explain why they were all summoned here on such short notice....

"As some of you may be aware, my only daughter, Princess Amiranda, has gone deep into the woods to try to find the man they call the Savant. No one is sure where this man is or if he actually even exists." King Jedrek stops for a moment, looking at one of the men directly in the eye. "What is sure is that the forest is a very dangerous place. For with the exception of this strange man who allegedly lives there, no one has ever entered the forest and come back out alive to tell about it," he tells them.

The king once again begins to pace, a million thoughts being deliberated in his mind as well as the visualization of what just might be happening to his daughter, the only heir to their throne. He continues …

"Now I know that this may be too much to ask from any one of you, but perhaps as a group we can find her and get her back safely. The entire kingdom is dependent on you. I, too, am humbly dependent. I am counting, nay, I am hoping on her quick and safe return."

Although normally a stern and strict man, for once King Jedrek is somewhat emotional, as he tries to do his best to cover up his concern for his daughter's welfare.

He continues, "Needless to say, there will be a handsome reward for those who accomplish this heroic feat of bravery and honor." He looks at the men, gazing upon them once again, seeking their help. "What do you say, are you up to the challenge good men?"

As the king waits eagerly for a reply, for the moment all is quiet. So quiet, in fact, that you can almost hear the rushed heartbeats of the men as they refrain from breathing; they are careful not to make a noise, or else their services may be mistakenly enlisted.

Moments pass, and then finally the king turns around and away from them, realizing that no one is willing to risk their own life for the sake of his daughter—that is, until one man speaks up.

"I will go." A voice simply calls out.

Quickly, King Jedrek looks to see the man who made the commitment. It is clearly surprising that only one person spoke up, as you can easily tell from the king's expression as well as the expression on Yule's face.

"I will go," the young man restates as he takes one step forward, distinguishing himself from the pack. The man may appear to be young, but still he is rugged, refined, and growing stronger with every day.

He is dressed handsomely, but his attire is very unassuming compared to that of the other men in the room. Whereas the other men are wearing clothing and garments clearly meant for warriors, this young man's attire look like it was designed for some sort of equestrian event. His leather boots also make him appear to be more like a stableman than a noble warrior.

"I will not require a reward either," the young man continues. "I will do it for the sake of our kingdom, the kingdom of Luxing," he proclaims, his voice still a bit shaky but still somewhat filled with conviction.

The king looks at the young stranger. He is clearly not the tallest of the group, nor the shortest, nor the fiercest looking or scrawniest either. However, he is the youngest. A young gentleman not too much older than Amiranda's age; he is perhaps one, maybe two years older, if that.

"What is your name young man?" King Jedrek earnestly asks.

"Adam," the young man replies simply. "My name is Adam."

The king is still somewhat taken aback that out of this whole group, only one man is willing to face the challenge, and yet all alone at that. King Jedrek addresses him directly.

"Adam, are you sure that you are up to such a challenge—all alone, mind you?"

Adam appears a little tense and a bit worried, but still he commits his services to the king. "I will go," he repeats himself.

"Very well, Adam," The king approves the brave young man's willingness, however futile it may be. "Anyone else?" he asks, as he looks around the room for more volunteers. Again, no one dares to make one move. Everyone remains silent and still as can be.

"Well, Adam, I commend you for your loyalty to the town and to our kingdom. May God be with you on your journey, and may he safely bring both you and my daughter home."

That being said, King Jedrek picks up a sword that is placed neatly on a royal pillow on his desk, perhaps protecting the desk, or perhaps protecting the sword itself. The sword appears to be made of a highly polished metal, perhaps sterling silver, and bears the royal coat of arms on both the weapon's handle and its razor sharp blade. The king lifts the heavy sword and presents it to Adam for the young man to take and keep with him on his journey.

"Take this sword and use it for protection," he tells him. "This sword was made from the salt of the earth, handed down for generations, and will help protect and guard you from danger."

Adam genuflects before the king and accepts the weapon, as well as the challenge to help save the princess. In his mind, he hopes that he has made the right choice.

With sword in hand, Adam gets ready to embark on his venture. He heads to his stable to ready the things he will need for his voyage—his satchel full of rations and provisions, a sheath for his sword, and, most importantly his horse, Whitetail.

Whitetail is a fine horse by anyone's standard, but even more so considering that Adam raised her since she was a small foal. Horse rancher by trade, the young man spent his whole life learning from his family how to train them, care for them, and even break them to ride. This is Adam's first attempt to take all that his family has taught him and to try to make a name for himself in the field. After all, horses are his passion in life.

Whitetail is, by far, his favorite of all the horses he has ever ridden or raised. She is faithful, obedient, swift, and strong. A purebred palomino, she is a beautiful mare; her colors are a mixture of a light brown and golden yellow. As her name clearly suggests, her tail is pure white, a rarity amongst the breed. Adam is very proud of her, and it shows.

As Adam saddles up, he begins to question himself about what it is he is doing. He does not know much of the forest he is about to enter, or of the young princess for whom he is searching, or even of the man he is seeking to find. In fact, it is pretty foolish of him to take on such a treacherous task. Yet, he is faithful to his town and the entire kingdom, as both have always done right by him. In his heart, he would like to somehow pay the royal family back for the freedom and the peace that he and his family were always allowed to experience and enjoy.

"Adam, what have you gotten yourself into this time?" he asks himself questionably. He has done crazy things before, but none of them ever as crazy as this. "Whitetail, I hope we both get our way through this," he tells her. She whinnies and nods her head, ready to obey his every command.

Without a second to lose, and not giving it another thought, Adam mounts his horse and gently snaps on the reins. He heads past the castle and straight into the forest, on a different trail than Amiranda traveled.

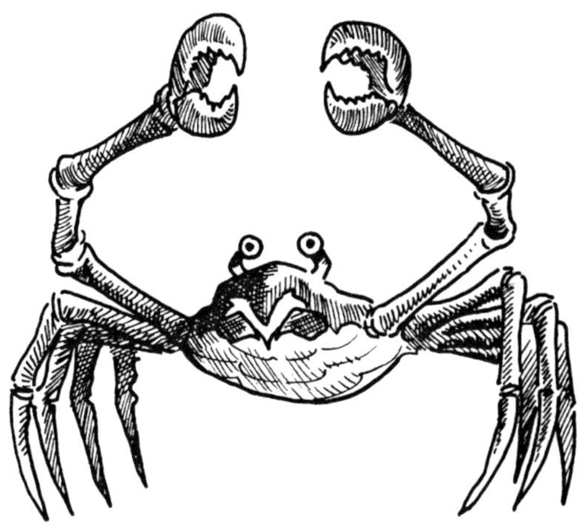

Chapter 15

The River Battle

With a sharp bellowing cry for their cavalry, the great masses of blowfish and fighting fish rush from the tranquil lake heading straight toward the turbulent river up ahead. All of them chant as they head downstream, the waters becoming more and more unforgiving as the lake funnels itself into a fast flowing river of hungry rapids. As the two armies of fish—literally hundreds and hundreds of them, continue downstream, they begin to enter the infamous spider crab territory. This is territory from which most would ordinarily choose to stay away.

Fervently, Amiranda pushes the raft along with the pole to try to keep pace with the vast organized mass of militia, following just behind the organized chaos of the fish as they are all ready to engage in battle. The raft and all those aboard begin to head downstream—somewhat uncontrollably.

As the wide river progressively begins to narrow, the current increasingly kicks in, acting up faster and faster. Huge boulders and sharp rocks get closer and closer to hitting the sides of the raft, endangering all those aboard as well as the already delicate raft itself. Amiranda's river stick with which she guides the raft ultimately becomes useless, except in trying to direct the craft away from any dangerous rocks.

Suddenly, and in one single and abrupt instant, the river becomes enraged as if someone or something was trying to make their journey all the more difficult. The translucent waters darken; they become dismal, murky, and dark due to the silt riverbed below churning up from the swift flowing current. The raft gets tossed and turned about every which way as everything becomes reckless and out of control. All those aboard do their best to hang on as Reynolds once again flies overhead, watching helplessly as the others risk their lives on the rickety raft. It is a tense moment for all as Amiranda tries desperately to steer clear of the rocks.

"What's happening?" Amiranda asks, stunned by the rapid change of the shifting waters. She raises her voice to overcome the noise of the swift current. Still, the noise almost drowns her out.

Simon shouts back to her, "Uh oh, he knows—you are near *his* territory."

The small and frail turtle holds on for dear life and anchors himself in order to try to stay afloat. Although he and Sigmund are good swimmers, the two of them would never survive in these hostile waters.

Amiranda's eyes widen. You can hear the fright hidden within her voice. "What?" she asks, "whose territory?" The princess continues trying to steer the raft clear of rocks as water splashes about, soaking everyone aboard. The raft rocks, rotates, and tilts around haphazardly; it is flung around like the bunch of twigs and branches tied together that they are.

"The evil Gispan," Simon replies. Amiranda was afraid he was going to say that, looking at him with her eyes becoming even more widened than before. "But he can't hurt you here. We're still a bit away."

"So what do we do?" Amiranda yells back, still trying to maintain control of the raft. Now it is more like she is trying to hold on rather than anything else. She clearly has no control of the raft or the turbulent waters, which effortlessly guide her farther and farther away from her home.

Once again showing his leadership and authority in a crisis situation, Sherman takes an upright stance at the bow of the craft. "Hold on!" he shouts all too simply before he himself retreats to the center of the vessel.

All those aboard were expecting a bit more from the fearless leader as they all immediately take heed to his orders. A huge wave splashes everyone aboard as the chaotic current acts up even faster. The raft starts heading straight down a steep dip in the river way, the white-water rapids being almost too much for the small raft to take.

Appearing far more greenish in color than usual, Sigmund pleads, "Is it too late to turn back now?"

They all reply in unison, "Yes!" Water flies everywhere. Sigmund retracts back into his shell.

The makeshift vessel's integrity slowly weakens as the fastening vines of the raft slowly loosen and unravel. With every hit of the rocks the raft takes, the ties come more and more undone. All onboard hope and pray that the bindings will hold together for just at least a little while longer as they all try desperately to hang on for their lives….

Meanwhile, just ahead of them, the group watches a sight almost impossible to believe. The two great armies of fish are now nearing their way to the rockiest part of the river—the notorious home territory of the infamously vicious spider crabs. Seamlessly, the conjoined forces of the blowfish army and the Japanese fighting fish army have become as one as they engage in a fierce battle against the much larger, villainous spider crabs. The blowfish begin to sing their infamous battle song …

Into the river,
Into the river,
Where waves get rough,
The going gets tough.

Into the river,
Into the river,
Where the seas grow strong
Is where we belong.

Side by side
Against the tide,
With all our might,
We will fight.

You and me,
One family
Against the tide;
We will survive.

Into the river,
Into the river,
Where waves crash down
All around.

We won't drown;
We will survive
Against the tide
Into the river.

The enemy is by far superior in both size and weaponry due to the spider crabs' armor-plated shells, their precision-motioned legs and their razor-sharp pinchers, which are truly massive in size—especially in comparison to their long and skinny legs. Each individual one alone is surely a formidable opponent with which to contend.

The spider crab's army is by far more fierce-looking than that of the brightly colored blowfish and Japanese fighting fish. They also perfectly blend into the background, being almost totally camouflaged in color. The only exceptions are the bright red stripes on their backs and pinchers, which make them look even more cruel and threatening. The markings are a testament to all of the former battles they have been on, and how many enemies they have destroyed. An organized militia of small fish is certainly no match for such a well-protected and perfectly designed war creature. Nonetheless, for Amiranda's sake, the two heroic armies of fish are determined to come out of this battle victorious.

Water is sprayed just about everywhere as the two mass armies of fish are jumping and fighting about every which way. They try their best to avoid the spider crabs' vicious and angry claws. The snapping sound of their pinchers closing tightly can be heard from miles away—sounding almost like firecrackers exploding in the distance. The spider crabs do whatever they can to try and overcome the two huge mass armies of blowfish and Japanese fighting fish surging relentlessly upon them.

The torrential waters crash against the rocks in the river, making it difficult for all to see. Amiranda loses sight of the fierce battle. She doesn't know which side is winning or which side is losing. Still, for the moment she has far more urgent things on her mind....

A binding in the raft suddenly unties and the crew loses a much-needed log from their raft. With the vessel now partially sinking, Sherman uses his claws, paws, and teeth to hold and tie the rest of the vines taught so that no more of it further unravels. Luckily, the group still manages to stay afloat, but just barely.

The princess turns to look at the melee. She still cannot see due to the constant spray of water and river foam splashing about. For a moment, everyone is silent, trying to hear any telltale signs of the battle up ahead. The only sounds than can be heard are the deafening roar of the rushing water nearby and the constant snapping of claws in the distance. Everyone waits with eager anticipation.

Finally, from within the clamoring noise of the battle, you can hear Shiro's voice announce, "Ah, we are too fast for you claw-snapping fools." The samurai leader proudly declares a small yet important victory.

The Japanese samurai leader is right. His group of fighting fish jumps through the claws of the spider crabs practically all unscathed, only to have the armored crustaceans hook onto themselves in their own efforts. Most of the ruthless crabs get trapped in their own web, in an endless maze of legs and claws all raveled, tied up, and twisted together.

The heroic efforts of the blowfish and the Japanese fighting fish are paying off—much to everyone's surprise. The blowfish inflate themselves, so that they are too large for the spider crabs' claws to get a hold of. In addition, the Japanesh fighting fish army is also more intelligent in their use of strategy and maneuvers compared to that of the spider crabs' army. It is a huge turning point in the conflict as Amiranda and her friends for once feel an ounce of hope in their efforts. Unfortunately for them, the battle isn't over quite yet....

Claws, the ominous leader of the spider crab army, is watching nearby. He sees his army beginning to lose the battle as they become more and more intertwined with one another. Being by far both the largest and most skillful of the spider crabs, Claws himself has somehow managed to maintain his ground, staying out of the mass entanglement of sharp and angry pinchers.

Heated over his own army's lack of ability and sheer incompetence, he shouts, "What are you waiting for? Get them you morons!" The menacing leader then turns to Amiranda and her friends and begins to head directly toward their raft. "I will get you for this!" he adamantly assures her, snapping his pinchers high up in the air.

The raft is now smack dead center in the midst of the heated battle. Surrounded by the army of spider crabs engaged in the struggle, Amiranda wards off the many crabs that are attempting to pirate her ship by using her river stick to swing at them. Still, she tries her best not to hurt any of them, she just wants to hold them at bay. Fortunately for her, Gordy's army of blowfish and Shiro's army of Japanese fighting fish are doing an excellent job of keeping most of the spider crabs preoccupied and off the vessel. The only exception is that of their leader, Claws, who cunningly manages to make his way onboard the raft.

The princess and her team retreat to the other side of the raft, trying to stay clear of Claws, the brutal spider crab leader. They stand at the far edge of the raft, that edge sinking more and more into the water. The menacing and vicious aggressor is advancing angrily toward them.

Closer and closer he moves near them, snapping his pinchers relentlessly and using all of his might in doing so. He has clearly had enough with these intruders. Amiranda tries to ward him off with her river stick, but Claws only cuts it into tiny pieces, shaving it off inch by inch. The princess gasps, not knowing what else to do.

Claws grins villainously. "Ah, I've got you now!" he snaps out loud. "The fight's not over yet." Slowly but surely he advances on the group, who are now all huddled together for protection. The villainous spider crab's razor-sharp legs poke into the wood like barbed spikes. They back up as far as they can go. All are leaning heavily on one side of the raft, almost tipping it over. Claws closes in on them, ready to strike.

Just then and all of the sudden, Peatie unpredictably, yet bravely, stands up to the much larger and far meaner king of the spider crabs. The small courageous pup steps forward and growls fiercely, or at least he tries for a puppy his size.

"Wait Peatie, No!" Amiranda tries to call him back to safety, but the small pup ignores her command, ever protective of his mistress. Claws, on the other hand, is only angered by Peatie's sheer determination, however futile it may be. He moves closer to the defenseless pup, snapping his pinchers all the louder as he prepares for combat.

Bravely, Peatie makes the first bold move by lunging and grabbing onto one of Claws' arms. He clamps down onto it with all of his might, shaking his head ferociously. Much to everyone's amazement, the small pup manages to hold his transgressor back, at least for the moment, as the spider crab is unable to grab hold of Peatie with his other claw. Amiranda watches helplessly as the two wrestle themselves into a ball, both of them equally holding their own ground.

Claws struggles violently, trying to release himself from the small puppy's hold. With his other arm, his razor sharp pincher manages to snip off a hair from Peatie's furry white tail. The two fighters skirmish around in circles as both try to gain the upper hand in battle. Still, the pup refuses to let go, no matter what the cost. With her hand cupped over her mouth, Amiranda looks on, watching and waiting anxiously. The rest of her animal friends chant the small pup on.

Just as the two are in the heat of their battle, accidentally they both plunge into the swift and fast moving current. Even while trying to stay afloat, they continue to wrestle as each is stubbornly trying to win the battle over the other. Amiranda gasps as she makes an attempt to grab Peatie from the turbulent current, but it is too late.

Quickly both her puppy and the villainous spider crab are completely out of sight, taken under by the force of the terrifying waters. Although they all look, they see no signs of Peatie, or even Claws for that matter. The raft quickly makes its way past the other fighting crabs and past the watery battleground. Although the battle may have been won against the wickedly evil spider crabs, the war itself may have been lost, as Peatie is nowhere to be found.

All is silent for a moment as all eyes are steadily transfixed on the lifeless waters. All that is heard is the continuous loud roar and wild rage of the rustling river, which surrounds them.

Reynolds flies ahead to see if he can locate his canine companion in the water as the current took him swiftly downstream. Although he was always jealous of the small pup, now he would give anything to see his little pal once again. Although Peatie is the newest member of the family, the small pup has always been like a brother to the parrot, even if they are of two separate species. The parrot quickly realizes that regardless of how much they may bicker or disagree, they will always be family. For the moment, his jealousy must be put aside in order to save him from the cold and deadly waters.

The raft continues to barely miss rocks by just a matter of inches; its bindings loosen with every impact of the reckless waves. For the moment, all seems hopeless.

Just then, the small pup's head pops up, but only for an instant. Peatie yelps for help as he struggles to stay afloat in the water. He tries to swim but is unable, being far too small for such large and violent waves. He begins to submerge once again.

Reynolds catches a glimpse of the distressed pup, marking his position in the water like an eagle with his laserlike precision. The courageous parrot daringly swoops down to save him without even a concern for his own welfare, far unlike how he typically behaves. With his beak, Reynolds manages to grab the small tuft of fur on the back of Peatie's neck, flapping his wings vigorously to try and stay aloft.

As Peatie is slowly taken out of the water, Claws manages to grab a tight hold of Peatie's tail. He clamps down onto it with all of his might.

The weight of carrying both Peatie and the menacing crab pulls Reynolds down, causing him almost to lose flight. Reynolds flaps his wings with all his might to stay aloft and to pull Peatie to safety, but Claws will simply not let go.

Unable to maintain control, Reynolds loses altitude and begins to fall—sending his two onboard passengers precariously close to the rocks and then partially back into the waters. Both Peatie and Claws are in danger of hitting one of the many the hard, secure, and unforgiving stones as they temporarily pass by them by unscathed. Although not planned or intended, the erratic flight pattern of the overstrained bird causes the spider crab to directly hit one of the boulders, thus sending him into the river where he belongs. Reynolds finally manages to pull Peatie swiftly up out of the water, carrying him safely aboard the raft.

"Peatie, are you okay?" Amiranda asks, thankful that he is now out of harm's way. Peatie is exhausted, and of course all soaking wet, but he is all right. "That was so brave of you," she pauses, turning to look at Reynolds; "both of you," she tells them. "Thank you."

Reynolds lifts his head high repeating, "Brave bird, brave bird; arrk." He shakes the water off of his feathers, at the same time flapping them proudly.

Unfortunately, there is no time for Amiranda and her friends to celebrate. Sherman chimes in yelling, "It ain't over yet!" He yells this just as everyone notices the waterfall they are just about to go over....

"Hold on everybody!" Simon shouts back, warning everyone to take heed as they are about to head straight over the falls. They all hold on to one another and anything else they can find on which to cling.

Sigmund retracts in his shell for cover. "I'll be in here if anybody needs me," he tells them, cowardly in his retreat.

Reynolds safely takes to the air for safety, but as for the rest, there is simply no turning away from the upcoming falls. He watches helplessly as the others plummet vertically over the steep edge of the watery cliff—deep into the almost bottomless river canyon below. He hears them yell as they fall into the abyss, their screams silencing as they vanish beneath him. Their cries are ultimately drowned out by the sound of the falling water. Reynold's heart nearly stops as he loses all sight of his friends. All he can see now is the mist created by the fall of the waters. For once, he is frightened, scared, and all alone.

As Reynolds continues to fly and circle overhead, all is eerily quiet. The only exception is the distant sound of white noise created by the powerful force of the waterfall. Ironically, it is almost heavenly where he is; it is a glorious day to be way up high in the sky—with the midday sun casting its light on his vibrantly beautiful and rainbow-colored wings.

For the first time in his life, Reynolds is like an eagle in the sky, soaring gracefully and flying effortlessly in the air. It is almost as though the small parrot is conquering the almighty heavens, something he has never before done. This is clearly something he is not used to—having spent most of his life locked up inside his cage. But it is something he could get used to, he undoubtedly thinks to himself. After all, the peace that exists way up here is quite opposite to that of the chaos looming below.

The parrot pauses; he is unsure of what to do. A multitude of questions enter his mind as he glides around peacefully in the air. Questions like: Should risk his own life; and if he did, would it do any good? Surely there was no chance the rest would have survived such a steep and disastrous

fall. And if they were not alright, would he really want to find out? The mist of the waters alone would weigh down his feathers, forcing him to plummet and fall like the rest, unable to take wing—thus sealing his own fate. Reynolds contemplates all of these things and more, remaining unsteady in his indecision.

The majestic bird circles above, looking down—hoping, but still not seeing any signs of Amiranda or the others. The misty spray of the water clouds everything below from view, and the image of the waterfall can be seen reflecting in the parrot's eye as he glides and soars overhead, as he is actively looking and listening for any telling signs of the others.

Although Reynolds is in midair for a matter of only seconds, still, to him it feels like an eternity. Quickly he realizes that it is lonely being on top, having no one else there who you can always turn to.

Finally, the forlorn parrot realizes that his friends are all he really has, and that their fate would be his own fate. With one quick swoop, he dives straight down after them—headfirst into the misty spray. His feathers are watered down by the mist as he falls and falls aimlessly for what seems like hours—right into Amiranda's lap.

"Nice of you to drop in on us," Amiranda laughs lightheartedly. "What took you so long?" She giggles; glad to see that Reynolds and everyone else is alright.

Reynolds, although happy to see everyone again, refuses to let on. "Very funny, warrk; very funny," he says both sarcastically and quite comically. Everyone laughs, as they are all overcome with joy. The group, now reunited, can continue on with their journey.

The mist from the waterfall gradually clears as the raft slowly drifts farther and farther away from the falls. Everything is much calmer here as the river becomes almost motionless, and all threats of the evil spider crabs are gone.

The raft, practically torn apart from the force of the fall, has its bindings all unraveled. Clearly, it has seen better days by far. Still, the vessel manages to stay aloft and keep all those aboard afloat. Gordy, the blowfish and Shiro along with the rest of the Japanese fighting fish suddenly all appear. They chant and rejoice in victory.

Amiranda praises the blowfish for their efforts; "Thank you, blowfish, for saving us—how ingenious of you to puff up like that to cushion us from our fall."

Reynolds now understands how they could have survived such a drop. If it were not for them, this surely would have been impossible.

She smiles at them continuing, "And thank you, Gordy, and Shiro, and friends for being so brave, and fighting so valiantly." They all smile.

The princess places her pup in her arms, holding him tightly, in gratitude for his courageous effort. "And thank you," she tells him, kissing him gently on the nose. Peatie licks her nose in return.

Last but not least, she turns to Reynolds, taking a moment as she looks at him ever so proudly. "You too, Reynolds," she tells him; "you are all heroes."

If ever a parrot could blush, now would be the time. For the first time in his life, Reynolds can regard himself as a true and genuine hero. He holds himself upright, standing tall and proud. Majestically, he spreads and flutters his wings as if to shake the water off of them, but more so to display his new found glory.

"Reynolds wants a cracker! Reynolds wants a cracker," he chimes eagerly.

"Alright, alright," Amiranda replies as she ruffles the feathers on top of his head so that they perk up once again. "—A *well-deserved* cracker," she kindly praises him.

The princess grabs a cracker from her pillowcase, which is also all soaking wet. Reynolds happily takes the soggy cracker, hungry as he is, but he accepts it more as a reward for a job well done. It is just then that Amiranda suddenly realizes the group has reached dry land. The rest of the journey will have to be carried on by foot; so it is time for her to part ways with her river companions.

Amiranda kneels at the edge of the riverbank, remaining close to the edge to say good-bye to her river friends who helped her come this far.

Gordy bids the princess and the rest a fond farewell.

"Hope all goes well for you Amiranda. If you're ever in the neighborhood, just whistle," he tells her. The brave leader then turns to his blowfish gang and tells them, "Okay guys, our job here is done. Let's go make fun of those spider crabs; I hear they are in a real pinch!" the blowfish leader laughs out loud, amused by his own play on words. Gordy gives one big smile to Amiranda, "Bye Amiranda! See you later, Shiro!"

Gordy and his army of blowfish submerge into the waters below, disappearing just as rapidly as they came. Amiranda and her friends wave to them all their good-byes, again wishing them well and thanking them for all of their help.

Shiro remains swimming beside the raft at the water's edge, along with the rest of his clan of Japanese fish-fighters, as they are the last ones to leave. You can see in his eyes that he knows that the time has come for him and his crew to depart. Amiranda and her animal friends must make the rest of their journey all alone.

"Aye, good-bye my friends," he respectfully bows before them in the water, clearly with the utmost admiration toward the travelers. "Remember to keep heart along your journey," he says reverently, sounding like some sort of ancient and wise Japanese proverb. A tear wells up in Amiranda's eye. "—and may the salt of the earth protect you from harm," he tells her.

The martial arts expert bows once again to the princess before swimming out of sight. He vanishes beneath the waters below, with his followers swimming swiftly behind him.

"Good-bye, Shiro. Thanks again," says Amiranda, once more a bit late in her reply. By now, Shiro is far below the surface of the waters. The young princess bows gracefully, grateful for their friendship and thankful for their assistance. Like a statue she stands there, waving to the vacant waters. Amiranda is lost in thought, vaguely remembering her mission. She wonders to herself if she will ever accomplish it. Once again, they are all alone, and in the middle of nowhere.

Amiranda leads the group a few feet ashore, unpacking her blanket for all to sit on and take a few minutes to rest. She prepares lunch for her heroes as they all share in the final remains of her leftover food.

Chapter 16

Shackled

A few miles behind Amiranda, Adam is on his horse surely making his way through the trail deep in the forest. Although it is midday, it is pitch-black where he is, as darkness surrounds him in almost every direction. This part of the woods is far more dangerous than where Amiranda currently is, as the mighty and evil Gispan controls every inch of this area of the strange, shadowy forest.

Adam begins to doubt his decision to take the more direct route, with the trail that leads him through the deep heart of the forest. Although he tries to travel at a swift pace, his horse, Whitetail, gets jittery with every small sound or sudden motion—whether it be the wind rustling the leaves, the snapping of the branches underneath her own hooves, or the swaying of branches as they precariously travel beneath them. The farther they travel, the harder it becomes for them to keep pace, for the path becomes quickly overgrown with bushy shrubs, thorny brambles, and entangling vines.

Suddenly, a chill inexplicably runs down Adam's spine. He can see the condensation of his horse's breath as she whinnies. She becomes even more jittery and troubled, as something peculiar and unseen is clearly upsetting her.

"It's okay girl," Adam tells her as he pats the side of the horse's neck, just below her mane. "I won't let anything happen to you, I promise."

The horse stops dead in its tracks, and her two front legs begin to fidget in place as they clip clop heavily against the stone-hard ground beneath her. She dares not move one step farther.

"Take it easy, Whitetail," Adam says to her in a gentle voice, trying to soothe her. Still, it is of no use.

Adam tries to urge her on with a squeeze from his legs and light tap on her reins, but Whitetail is unable to calm down. She stops responding to her master's command. Adam can sense something terribly wrong as well, feeling a tingle as the hairs stand at the back of his neck. He has never felt this way before nor has he ever seen his horse act this way, having raised her ever since she was a young mare.

Adam dismounts his horse. While still holding tightly to the reins, he slowly positions himself in front of the animal, taking one step closer to the coldness before them. Again, he pats his horse, this time rubbing the bridge of her nose to help calm her. Now, Adam can see his own breath as the chilled air blowing in from the front of them touches his face. He holds very still.

Suddenly, Adam feels something happening beneath his feet. He looks down and begins to see small fragments of the dirt below begin to move and separate from one another. From out of the ground, he watches as small sprouts begin to quickly grow and vastly multiply. Almost immediately, the shoots turn into vines that are grabbing at his ankles.

The brambles and branches around him connect with his arms, and begin to take hold of him. He quickly grabs his sword out of its sheath, but his movement is restricted by the growing plants and he is unable to move it. The vines twist around his legs, shackling him in place. Adam is unable to move.

The same vegetation begins to grab at Whitetail, but somehow she manages to buck and break her way loose just in time. She tramples the vines and branches with her heavy hooves, trying to restrict and restrain them.

Taken by surprise and no longer able to control her, Adam lets go of his horse's reins, allowing her to escape and move freely. Whitetail does not know what to do. She wants to remain loyal and stay by her master, but if she were to do this, they both would become entangled by the forest plants and surely die.

"Hurry, Whitetail, run!" Adam commands her. Whitetail whinnies again, this time louder than the first. Still, she remains with her master, appearing bewildered and confused as to what to do. She continues to stomp on the vines and even chew at the ones holding Adam to set him free, but it is a losing battle. There is nothing she can do.

"It's okay, Whitetail, go!" Adam yells at her. Having no other winning alternative, the horse quickly gallops off—running away from the eerie coldness and mysterious presence that lurks directly in front of her master….

Barely able to move his arms and legs, the vines have inexplicably taken ahold of Adam. Instantly, they turn from a bright, fleshy and lively green, to a dark, rough and lifeless brown, holding him steadily in place. His hands are still free to move, but that does nothing to help him free himself, even though he still clutches his sharp sword. In the darkness before him, glowing red eyes appear from behind the brush.

"Who's there?" Adam asks, still trying to shake his legs to break free. "I mean you no harm," he explains. Adam knows that it is something out of the ordinary with which he is dealing. He believes it to be the one responsible for controlling the vines.

From behind the brush, a smoky black figure of a man appears. The dark, shadowy outline of his mysterious black horse can be seen in the background. Gispan stands directly in front of the young man, smiling as he taunts the young intruder's poor soul. The coldness given off by the strange villain is practically unbearable to Adam.

"Who are you?" Adam demands. "I promise you, I mean you no harm. Let me go!"

The evil sorcerer takes a step toward the young man, closely inspecting him. Obviously, this "hero" poses no threat to his master plan. After all, there is no one who can stop his diabolical evilness from unfolding.

"So you are the one who they sent," Gispan states proudly, "how very interesting." He interlaces and locks his fingers, fidgeting and folding them up as he contemplates everything in his mind. His golden staff is hanging in place at his side, with the blue sapphire crystal that rests atop it almost mesmerizing Adam.

"What do you want from me?" Adam demands, as he is still trying to break loose from the rock-hard solid grip of the vines. The harder he tries to break free, the tighter the hold becomes.

"No," Gispan answers, "it is what you want from me that is important."

"I do not ask anything of you, just let me go," Adam demands once again. He begins to relax, knowing that the more he tries to break free, the harder it becomes for him to breathe.

"This is my land, this is my forest, therefore I will make the decisions," Gispan replies, firmly showing that it is he who is in control, as the vines endlessly tighten and grow further around their prisoner.

"I am only here to help," Adam replies, hoping that the dark, shadowy stranger will let him go. "I have come to help save a lost girl," he says carefully, suspicious of the frightening stranger.

It is clear that Adam does not know the tale of the forest or the story of the mighty and evil Gispan who stands before him; all he knows is that this is no place for any man to be.

"You mean young Amiranda, the princess," the evil villain tells him, already knowing why Adam is here. "It is too late for you now, as there is no escape for her. She is deep within my forest—just where I want her." Gispan's smile widens.

"I don't understand," the young man replies.

"You simple-minded fool. It is I who put a spell on the young princess' Nana, to get the princess to come here in the first place."

"What? You caused that? But why?" Adam tries to break free of the vines' hold once again, but clearly it is of no use.

"Because she represents all that is good and pure in the kingdom. Without her, the entire kingdom will suffer and be destroyed. Then I can rule it all!"

Adam feels the shock of the bizarre logic behind the evil villain's plan as it still makes no sense to him. Struggling to break free, the young man cannot help but question the dark shadow's radical, erratic reasoning.

"What did they ever do to you? Why would you want to destroy their family? Their dynasty? Their kingdom? They have done nothing but good."

"That's just it. They do nothing but good," the dark villain answers. "How upsetting it is to me. She is the last heir to the kingdom, and the purest of all. Since my evil magic will not work on her, I will have it bring her directly to me. Neither you, nor anyone else can stop me!" The shadowy villain laughs a bone-chilling laugh that cuts deep down into Adam's soul.

Then as fast as the sorcerer first appeared, Gispan vanishes into midair, leaving Adam standing there still shackled and unable to move.

The villain's horse disappears as well, but instead of evaporating into midair like his master, he runs off into the distance, quickly blending in with the dark, black forest background. The sound of his heavy hooves trampling onto the soil below can be heard as they gradually fade farther away.

Although he is left trapped and all alone, initially Adam does not lose all sense of hope. He struggles hard to try and break free, not allowing the wicked sorcerer to get the best of him ... not yet, anyway. After time and time again, he clearly sees it is of no use as the shackle-like plants just cling onto him ever stronger.

Trapped within the vines, Adam cannot escape the bindings nor do anything about Gispans' diabolical plan. Like the others who went into the woods before him, the young man is left to die there, cold and all alone. He came here to help rescue others, but now the tables have turned as there is no one around who can help rescue him.

Chapter 17

The Savant

After eating their lunch and resting for a while, Amiranda and the group travel farther into the woods along a deep, dark trail. The more they move away from the river, the more unnerving the forest appears, once again becoming lifeless and dismal. It is late afternoon now, and all are getting more and more worried as the day itself grows darker, and their shadows grow longer. All are wary of their surroundings, checking every which way as they cautiously proceed along the winding path.

Simon whispers, "I hope we're getting close."

Sherman replies nervously, "We are getting close." The frigid weather augments the shakiness in his already uneasy tone of voice. "For this is where I last saw Gispan."

Just as he utters Gispan's name, the forest around them instantly transforms, growing much colder. The abrupt change in temperature sends chills up and down the travelers' spines. They bundle themselves in their own arms to keep warm as the leaves start to fall lightly among them.

Amiranda is perplexed by the strange shift in weather. "I thought it was supposed to be spring?" she asks herself.

"Now can I go back?" Sigmund questions, once again displaying his eagerness to abandon the quest.

"NO!" All reply in unison.

Although some fear the worst, still, Amiranda remains hopeful. She leads the group steadily, but much more cautiously through the deep dark woods. It is all in hopes of finding the Savant, but she is still uncertain if he can, or perhaps even will, help.

As the group journeys farther and farther into the woodlands, the weather continues to worsen. The wind picks up, the skies grow cloudy and dark, and a cold, dismal rain begins to fall. The princess picks up her pup, vigilant to protect him from the chill, and quite unsure if they are all headed in the right direction. All she knows is that she is a long, long way from home and her warm, comfortable bed.

After almost an hour's worth of traveling, they eventually see a small flickering light up ahead. The faint glow in the distance is quite a sight for sore eyes. Instinctively, they all decide that they should make their way toward the light's soft and almost comforting glow—actually, it is all they have to travel by. However, the closer and closer they get to it, the more the wind acts up. The blustery breeze blows directly against their faces, almost stopping the group dead in their tracks. Amiranda senses that something, or perhaps even someone, does not want them there. Despite the apparent warning, the group edges onward, determined to reach the light.

Bit by bit, through the dark foliage and dense brush before them, they begin to piece together the outline of a small structure from whence the glow is emanating. As they draw closer, they see that it is from a candle's flame flickering from inside a small window. Now at last, they see that there is a small cabin in the distance.

Amiranda whispers, "Is … this … the … place?" She is hesitant in her question, already knowing the answer. Her whisper is loud enough for all to hear, especially over the loud wind that is starting to howl, but still soft enough to try not to let anyone else hear—especially Gispan.

"This is the place," Simon replies.

The wind practically pierces through the weary voyagers' souls. So far it has been a treacherous journey for only a day's worth of travel. And although the voyage to find the Savant may be near over, the ultimate journey's end is still nowhere in sight.

Amiranda leads the animals to the front porch of the log cabin. Although the cabin is rundown by age, weather, and neglect, Amiranda can tell the structure must have been quite a quaint dwelling back in its heyday. She can see the remnants of fine craftsmanship all around—from the custom woodwork around the windows to the scrollwork trimming the porch, from the joining of the logs that were married together with exacting precision to how the posts of the porch were ornamentally handlathed with such uniform accuracy. Overall, the size of the dwelling is quite small, cozy, and inviting; it is far unlike Amiranda's much larger, more lavish, and relatively intimidating palace, which she calls "home."

As the princess lightly treads to the door, the floorboards of the porch that were loosened and warped by years of rain and neglect creek eerily beneath her. Her animal friends keep their distance just behind her, cautious to stay at her heels. Each one of them keeps an eye both on the door and all around them for safety. Without any further delay, she knocks on the door both politely yet anxiously.

"Hello, is anyone here?" the princess asks in a loud whisper, trying to let her voice overcome the howling wind, yet trying not to be too loud to be a disturbance in case their company is not welcome. Amiranda looks around, noticing two heavy gray stones precariously placed on one side of the porch's steps—one large and the other one smaller. She thinks to herself that they look like the ones in Simon's story....

Just then, interrupting Amiranda's own thoughts, the door handle slowly turns. The animals gasp and Sigmund retreats back into his shell for protection, even more scared than usual, and this time rightfully so. Little by little the door begins to swing inward, letting out a blustering squeak as it opens ever so slowly. In the doorway stands a shadow of a man, his facial features blackened out by the faint shimmer of light peeking out from behind him. The group inches back, unsure if the strange man is a friend or foe.

It takes a moment for Amiranda's and her friend's eyes to adjust to the changing light. As the stranger slowly steps back, allowing the door to open wider and wider, gradually they begin to see more of him. The flickering candle in the background increasingly illuminates his face.

The stranger is a fairly rugged, yet still relatively handsome, middle-aged gentleman. He appears to be slightly grizzly in appearance, having a medium length golden-brown beard and moustache, perhaps a result of being stranded in the middle of the woods all this time. His appearance almost matches the appearance of the cabin—brown, disheveled, and somewhat rundown. The stranger smiles; this slightly eases Amiranda's anxiety, at least for the moment.

"My, I don't get much company around here," he confesses, yet not all too surprisingly. Remarkably, it seems as though he is expecting them. For Amiranda, this seems quite unusual, since it is obvious that no one has been this way in ages. Still, she has come a long way, and this is the only sign of human life she has seen for miles.

"Please come in, come in," the welcoming stranger offers. He kindly motions them inside with one arm as he holds the door open for them with the other. Amiranda graciously accepts, watching carefully as she leads the others inside.

The princess looks around, noticing and analyzing everything around her, the way she often does when it comes to any new surroundings she encounters. She has always been inquisitive, and yearning to learn more. Although anxious, tired, and concerned, her true behavior this time proves to be no different than at any other time.

The cabin inside has a simple floor plan, with the front entryway directly opening into one large living space. Small and quaint as the structure is, this larger room is offset by two smaller rooms along the far wall, perhaps one for a bed and the other for a bath. The walls themselves are plain, as the natural color of the wood logs makes up the structure forming them. Nevertheless, the inside of the cabin seems very warm and welcoming—especially for these parts of the woods where everything else is very cold, harsh, and inhospitable.

Oddly enough, occupying one half of the main room are all sorts of chemistry materials, which are set up on top of a worktable. Numerous flasks, vials, beakers, and burners are filled with different amounts of colorful potions all across the room—perhaps part of some sort of chemistry experiment. Some liquids are changing color continuously, others are giving off some sort of smoke or steam, and still others appear to be boiling over. Amiranda is so intrigued by the whole setup that it takes a few moments before she notices anything else in the room.

Set off to the farther half of the cabin, there is a small dining table neatly lined with some small wooden chairs, just adjacent to the cabin's kitchen. It is quite a strange combination to have a chemistry experiment taking place right next to the kitchen. This gives Amiranda all the more reason to believe that the stranger is the man for whom she has been searching.

"You must be Amiranda," the stranger says, much to her amazement. He offers out his hand for her to shake, and after a moment's deliberation she graciously accepts. "And how are you guys? Are you hungry?" he asks, showing genuine concern for his guests. "I just cooked dinner." Again, much to their surprise, they see some food already prepared and set out for them.

"You must be the man they call the Savant," she tells him, questioning him at the same time. "But how did you know I was coming?"

"Call me Jamarcus." The clairvoyant stranger's reply is simple and quite modest, perhaps in an attempt to de-emphasize his own importance. Although the mysterious man is still a stranger, the princess and the rest of her group slowly start to warm up to him as he seems to mean them no harm.

"Hello, Jamarcus," Amiranda curtsies, either out of habit or possibly due to her royalty; but most likely because she cannot permit herself to do otherwise—a result of her strict upbringing. Not letting go of her original question, she asks, "So how did you know my name?" As always, whenever she asks a question, she is determined to get a suitable answer in response.

Jamarcus gently leans in toward the young princess, so he can talk to her more personably; he is physically close to her. Amiranda knows that she should be frightened by such an imposing presence, but still she senses a genuine nobility and graciousness dwelling deep within him. By simply looking at him she can feel the intensity of his kindness. His deep-set, rugged eyes, shadowed beneath his strong brow practically mesmerize the young princess.

The candle's steady flickering illuminates the stranger's eyes in steady flashes of light, adding great dimension to his many rugged and strong features. The uneven curve of his jawline, the jagged edges of his cheekbone, and the sorrowfulness displayed within each soft wrinkle of his face whenever he smiles, all play a part in Amiranda's admiration of the gracious stranger. Even without a single word being said by him, she can clearly tell that he is wise beyond his years.

"Oh, Amiranda," he finally tells her, "It need not be explained, only understood." His response avoids the question altogether, as his voice answers with a mystical tone of wisdom. It is clearly evident to her that these are simple words with a far more complex meaning. "Now, shall we eat before you set off again on your journey? I have prepared this meal especially for you. All of you must be famished."

Jamarcus seats Amiranda at the table like a true gentleman ought;

he first pulls out her chair and then gently places it under her as she sits. To her delight, a meal is already set out in the middle of the table before her. There is succulent flame broiled meat cooked to perfection, mouthwatering mashed potatoes with homemade gravy, cooked peas and carrots, and other side dishes, including freshly baked bread. It is a meal truly fit for a king—or in this case, a princess.

The hospitable stranger kindly places the food on some plates for Amiranda and her animal friends. He sets out a bowl filled with puppy food for Peatie, two adjacent plates of salad for Sigmund and Simon, and a dish filled with a mixture of berries and nuts for Sherman. After helping them with their servings, he then gently coaxes Reynolds to climb onto his shoulder so as to feed him by hand. Reynolds is far too famished to turn down the offer of this inviting man. Jamarcus seems to know practically everything about them—their likes, their tastes, their individual behaviors—everything.

He gives Sherman another helping of finely chopped acorns and wild nuts. "How's that my furry friend?" he asks Sherman the squirrel. "I picked them just for you."

Sherman replies with delight, "Oh my, why that's just lovely, just lovely." It is unclear whether or not Jamarcus understands the squirrel's response the same way Amiranda can. What is clear is how Sherman begins to devour his meal ravenously, as anyone can truly understand. Amiranda continues to question the stranger, in hopes that he will be able to help her.

"So you know the reason I've come?" the princess asks as she politely yet graciously helps herself to some more of the food set out before her. Amiranda cannot refuse his offer either. As Jamarcus rightfully pointed out, she is nearly famished, having not eaten a real meal in almost two days, let alone a good home cooked meal like this one.

Unknowingly, Amiranda ravenously devours her whole meal. Still, she remains somewhat successful in trying to maintain her dignified, noble poise. The princess has grown accustomed to Kistoffe's so-called "Franch" cuisine back home, and as a result, has grown tired of the same meals day after day. This is certainly a tasteful treat for her in her "mouthwatering" request for a change. She politely wipes her mouth with a napkin, carefully covering her mouth, which is, by the way, still partially filled with food. Everyone is happy, and full.

Immediately after dinner, Jamarcus takes a step closer to his homemade laboratory. Amiranda and her friends were too busy eating to notice or remember to ask about the strange items in his cabin. The Savant rifles through the assortment of liquid-filled beakers and other strange apparatuses, finally grabbing a particular vial.

"I have the potion you need for your Nana right here," he explains as he holds up a blue flask containing an even bluer potion inside. He stares at it closely, swirling the mixture around in front of the light, carefully watching the liquid churn inside.

"That one was easy," he continues explaining. "I mean after many years of research that is," Jamarcus quickly corrects himself. By the way he is speaking, Amiranda can tell that there is a certain heaviness still felt deep in the stranger's heart. He breathes a heavy sigh. "Now if I can only find the one *I* need," he says remorsefully. He looks down at the floor beneath him, his mind racing as it goes over all the solutions he has tried. Unfortunately, none of them have worked.

"Do you know if there is such a potion?" Amiranda inquires, already knowing to what Jamarcus is referring. Filled with empathy for the kind stranger, the princess temporarily forgets the fact that the man has the remedy her Nana needs; she now shows more concern for Jamarcus' own well-being than her own personal desires and wishes.

Jamarcus takes a step closer to the window, looking out into the dark, mysterious woods where the grassy green meadow once used to exist many, many years ago. Now, he can barely tell the forest from the trees, as the two have become one—completely interwoven, almost like mangrove trees trying to suffocate one another. For him, the endless mesh of roots is everywhere and purely inescapable. Every time he would cut a branch or clear a tree, at least six more would soon follow. Oh, how he yearns to be able to work out in the fields again, working as his wife and son look at him from that very same window.

Deeply pondering Amiranda's question, he thinks and remembers how things were, and how things ought to be. Calmly, he softly strokes the tip of his chin, contemplating the question over and over again in his mind.

"There must be such a potion," he says, halfway underneath his own breath. "There just simply must be," the Savant repeats himself even softer this time, "but I haven't seen it." For a moment, the man's voice suddenly loses all sense of hope.

Then, just as quickly, if not even quicker, Jamarcus abruptly turns to Amiranda, gazing deep into her eyes. Determinedly he declares, "The evil sorcerer Gispan said that there was a potion, and I'm going to stay here until I find it!" The Savant's inner spirit seems to be once again renewed; his heart is filled with vigor to succeed in this difficult, if not impossible, conquest. Perhaps it is all too late....

All of a sudden, in that very same moment, the ground begins to rumble, ever so lightly at first, but then it grows more powerful and violent. The flasks, vials, and beakers all begin to rattle and shake. The trembling becomes deeper and deeper, as if there is some sort of an earthquake happening all around them. Finally, one of the vials falls to the floor and breaks, letting out a loud crash. There is no doubt about it; Gispan must have heard him call out his name.

"Hurry, you must go swiftly!" Jamarcus exclaims. He begins to close the shutters of the cabin for protection. A horse's crying neigh, much like the one in Simon's story, is heard just outside the cabin. Amiranda recalls that story all too well, reliving it in her memory frame by frame.

Jamarcus realizes that the danger is too close upon them. The shutters are barely closing due to the wind picking up ferociously. Leaves fly in as he tries to wrestle them shut. Worried for Amiranda's safety he shouts "It's too late! Take cover!"

Amiranda and her animal friends all jump to their feet as they begin to retreat to the far side of the room for safety. For added protection, the animals all huddle and line up behind the princess, cowering in fear over the phenomenon of sheer evil power overcoming the woods. Things begin to fall all around them—pictures off of walls, dishes out of cupboards, drinking glasses off the table. With each crash they hold on to one another closer and closer.

Suddenly, the cabin door mysteriously swings itself wide open, clanking loudly as it hits against the back wall of the doorframe. Everyone gasps as a mysterious dark blue fog slowly creeps through the doorway.

"You are not welcome here. Leave now!" Jamarcus yells at the entity. He places himself in front of his laboratory equipment and his visitors, spreading his arms out wide, safeguarding all of them equally.

The strange fog enters the room, slowly filling it, gradually encompassing everyone and everything. For a moment, they can see nothing around them but sheer darkness. Then, through the mist of the haze, finally appears the fiery glow of Gispan's yellowy-reddish demonlike eyes.

As fast as it appeared, the haze quickly dissipates around the invading intruder. The shadowy silhouette of his dark, distinct outline and the long staff he is holding is revealed. The mighty and evil Gispan is, by far, more wicked and mean-looking than anyone had envisioned or remembered him to be. Amiranda and her friends gasp; they are frightened by the sorcerer's discernable figure standing in the doorway. Peatie, protective of his mistress Amiranda, courageously growls at the tall villain.

In a deep, dark, and fiendish tone, Gispan denounces Jamarcus. “You couldn’t leave well enough alone,” he tells him. “Against my better judgment, *I* decided to *let* you stay here and fool around with your silly little potions. *Now* you have the gall to try to help the small girl who dares to challenge my evils?”

The mighty and evil Gispan reaches out and grabs the vial filled with blue potion from Jamarcus—the very same potion that Jamarcus said was specially made to cure Amiranda’s Nana. Violently he throws it to the floor, watching it break into a million pieces. He laughs maniacally. “Now what are you going to do, little Amiranda?” he taunts her.

The liquid from Jamarcus’ potion spreads across the cabin’s floor. For some reason the chemical mixture of the potion spreading across the wood floor combined with the exposure to the air causes the liquid to begin to boil and smoke. After a moment, the smoke suddenly bursts into flames, instantly igniting the wood floor below. Jamarcus knows if he lets his guard down and moves to try to put out the flames, they all will be at risk.

Rapidly the flames spread, quickly burning the laboratory table itself. As the flames grow larger, they start to cause a chain reaction with the other potions, heating and igniting the flasks one by one. Steadily, the cabin becomes engulfed in a sheer blaze of insatiable fire.

The evil Gispan laughs, standing proudly in the doorway with his arms folded, his staff resting firmly against his chest. He shows no fear, himself having none; he knows that little Amiranda and her diminutive friends are of no challenge to his sheer wicked power. There is nothing that they can do to stop him.

With little or no concern for his own safety, Peatie quickly darts at the shadowy figure, trying to attack him by tugging and tearing at his pants' leg. It is a brave yet comedic effort to thwart the villain, given the puppy's small size in contrast to Gispan who stands there invincibly.

Unlike the spider crab, Claws, the small pup is no match for the wicked sorcerer, both in size, strength, and ability. This time Peatie is way out of his league—Gispan does not even realize his puny and insignificant little presence.

Instantly, the maniacal villain vanishes before their eyes, leaving only a puff of black smoke still in the air. Besides the growing flames, it is the only remaining telltale sign and lingering evidence proving that the evil villain was even there at all. It is a sight that must be seen to be believed.

Amiranda and her friends have never seen such dark black magic before. The small pup is bewildered by the mysterious disappearance, still yelping at the remaining smoke. Then, in the distance, the distressing cry of Gispan's mighty horse is heard—just like the one envisioned and heard in Simon's tale. It is shortly followed by the horse's hoofsteps riding off, fading as they travel farther and farther away.

Grabbing the tablecloth in an attempt to put out the flames, Jamarcus quickly swats at the fire. Unfortunately, it is of no use. The flames spread even faster, fueled by the oxygen given off by the upward and downward motion of the cloth. They only grow brighter and hotter.

"Quick, get out!" he yells.

Everyone heads out of the flaming cabin, and all run to safety, except for Jamarcus who stays behind for some inexplicable reason. Amiranda yells out to him, "Come on!"

Still, Jamarcus remains behind. Looking back, the princess watches as he exits his cabin only to remain standing in front—still in harm's way. He seems to be staying by the stones, trying to move the larger, heavier one. "Come on!" she urgently repeats herself. Neither the stones nor Jamarcus himself are budging.

"Come on!!!" she pleads now in desperation. Amiranda's words are no source of encouragement for Jamarcus who is determined not to leave the stones behind.

Smoke billows from the cabin, which is becoming overwhelmed with flames. Then suddenly, the mixture of burning chemicals creates a small explosion, which causes the shutters to blow right off of the building. As the blaze shoots from the window, it nearly touches Jamarcus who remains practically within its reach. Nevertheless, he is determined to stay, holding onto both of the stones ever so tightly.

"I can't leave my family," Jamarcus declares in sheer exasperation. The flames grow closer and closer. The heat felt from the fire is so blistering hot that Amiranda can hardly maintain her proximity to the cabin—the scorching blaze is almost unbearable. Jamarcus tries even harder to move the stones with every ounce of strength he has. Still, the stones won't budge.

"I won't leave my family!" he yells again, but this time his yell is directed at the surrounding air. Using all the strength held within his voice, he is hoping the evil Gispan will hear him. Adamantly, he shakes his fist in the air in the direction the wicked villain and his black demonic horse were last heard traveling. Having already completed the sinister task they were set to accomplish, they are nowhere to be found.

For once, all hope is lost. It seems as though the kind Savant has ultimately been defeated. Jamarcus' wife and son remain embedded in stone, his cabin is completely engulfed in flames, and the potions have been lost in the blaze. Even Amiranda's potion is gone—the one she so desperately needs for her sick Nana. Now she does not know what she is going to do. In short, everything good has been completely conquered by evil.

As the cabin's inferno continues to burn even closer and hotter to Jamarcus and his family who are embedded within the stone, the distraught man begins to cry. With his head and cheek placed firmly against the stones and his arms wrapped securely around them, be begins to weep on the stones—*something he never did before*. The tears steadily drip down from his eyes. With such sorrowfulness, love, and compassion they fall. Softly they descend onto the larger stone, and then from the larger, they trickle down to the smaller one. The princess just watches, she is unable to do or say anything that would make him turn away and leave his family.

Suddenly, a transformation happens—a sheer and undeniable miracle.

The blue-gray stones somehow magically change and transform back into his wife and son, exactly as he remembers them. They are both still young in age and both still waiting for him lovingly. Overcome with joy, Jamarcus gives his newly reborn family a short-lived yet wholehearted hug before they run to safer ground. Not a second too soon either; the cabin collapses, swiftly surrendering to the fire.

At last all are safe, at least for the time being. The very same spot where the cabin used to stand is now a pile of smoldering ash and useless rubble. Still, Jamarcus is jubilant. He does not care about the cabin, his home, his laboratory, or anything else for the moment; he is just happy to see his wife and son, as they are both alive and breathing again. For years and years they have been trapped in stone, tortured by Gispan's evil and magical power.

Speaking mostly to himself, Jamarcus affirms, "Of all the magical potions I have tried, I never tried love."

Tears continue to fill and flow from his eyes. They are watery tears that show the Savant's undying devotion to his family. Jamarcus stands there looking deep into the faces of his dear wife and son, remembering and reliving each joyful moment they loved and shared together. He cradles both of them in his arms, rocking them back and forth softly.

In the near distance, Amiranda watches silently. From where she stands, she sees the dark silhouette of the Savant and his family holding one another tenderly, fixed against the blazing background of the burning fire. Although she cannot help but feel happiness for the Savant and his newly reunited family, at the same time the princess remains equally disappointed that she did not receive the cure her Nana so desperately needs.

Seeing the cabin go up in smoke, Amiranda quickly realizes that all hope to save her Nana has gone up in flames as well. Just like the Savant, Amiranda's eyes well up with tears. However, instead of tears of joy like Jamarcus has, Amiranda's tears are filled with sadness. Still, she is careful not to allow herself cry.

Regaining his composure, Jamarcus squeezes his wife one last time before letting go. Suddenly he turns his head to Amiranda.

"Oh, by the way" he tells her, "here's the potion you really need." Jamarcus gently pulls out a small vile from his shirt pocket. However, this vial contains a strange, bright green-colored liquid, and not the blue potion as originally thought by Amiranda to be the cure. Somehow, the Savant knew all along that the evil Gispan would destroy the other vial.

Amiranda runs to him with her arms wide open. She hugs him graciously and he spins her around in his arms. "Oh, thank you, thank you ever so much," she says as the tears now begin to flow from her eyes. Now joyful and overcome with emotion, she cannot restrain them any longer.

Jamarcus stares gratefully into his wife's loving eyes, capturing visions of the moment. "No Amiranda, *thank you*," he emphatically replies.

Before everyone has the time to finish thanking one another, the ground begins to shake again. However, this time it is more fervently than ever felt before....

"We gotta get out of here!" Jamarcus urgently tells everyone. "Come on guys, I've got a plan. Follow me!"

With conviction, the Savant leads the group away from where his cabin used to stand. He assures the princess and her friends that he has a ready-made strategy, although most of it was just conceived, and all of it is far from being certain. He, nor anyone else for that matter, can be confident that Gispan can even be defeated at all.

Everyone follows him deeper and deeper into the darkening woods and farther away from Amiranda's home.

Chapter 18

The Wicked Plan

Adam, still bound by the vines which secure him, is growing tired, frail, and weak. He is still holding his sword, but can barely lift it any longer. He tries to position it toward one of the vines, hoping to cut a piece of it, but is still unable to do so. It is a losing battle.

Exhausted and disheartened, he has given up all hope. He cannot bear the pain of holding the sword any longer, even though it is his only means of defense. Still, the sword proves meaningless since he cannot even swing the weapon. Uncontrollably, Adam drops the sword to the ground. As he releases it, the sword falls deep into the ground, piercing the dirt and burying the tip of the blade within the soil. He tries to grab at the sword but cannot, as its handle is now well out of reach. Alas, he is left there to die.

Then, Adam watches as something entirely unbelievable begins to happen. The part of the sword that entered the earth causes the vines around it to wither, die, and decay. After a few moments, some of the plants quickly turn to dust—those that are closest to the metal. Adam finally realizes that the sword can most likely defeat the vines of the forest, if not in fact, the evil villain himself. That is, if he can free himself first.

As the vines around the sword continue to wither, the bindings around his arms and legs slowly begin to loosen, allowing him to eventually break free of their tight hold. It is still some struggle for Adam to do so, but ultimately he manages. Shaking and brushing the remaining debris off of himself, he lifts the sword out of the ground. He is surprised by the strangeness of it all.

Slowly he waves the sword in front of him, observing every part of it carefully, curious over its mystical power. It appears to be a normal sword, showing no signs of higher purpose or magical strength. Then, with great vigor he takes a swing at the vine closest to him—it is a thick and heavy plant. The same thing happens—the sword's metal cuts through the foliage like hot forged steel slicing through paper.

Adam takes a swing at another vine, and then another one. Those too, quickly shrivel up and wither away, for every part of the forest that comes in contact with the sword stands no chance against its supreme command. He also realizes that he does not have to swing hard to get the same result, as all of the branches and vines quickly succumb to this powerful weapon.

Filled with renewed vigor, the young rescuer quickly regains his composure, ready to continue his trek. He continues to head down the path and then begins to chop down pieces of the forest, creating his own way in which to travel.

Adam rapidly makes some progress toward the group, as he is almost running farther into the forest, all the while cutting every branch, vine, and small tree that blocks his way. He still does not know how far off Amiranda and the Savant are, or if he will be able to catch up to them in time to help save them. He knows that he must try. Now that he has both the strength and the knowledge to do so, he must give it his best shot.

Suddenly, after traveling quite some distance, he feels that same strange sensation he felt before as an eerie cold numbness comes over him. He stops dead in his tracks, his sword held directly in front of his face; he scans his surroundings from side to side, left to right. The air from his breath condenses against the sword's metal, appearing every time he exhales and disappearing every time he inhales. Slowly, he takes one step back, positioning himself in a clearing away from any brush or vines that may grow and grab hold of him again.

In the near distance, he hears the harsh cries of a wild horse as it neighs, whinnies, and moans violently. Knowing every sound ever to be made by his own horse, Whitetail, Adam realizes that this is definitely not her. Also familiar with each and every sound made by any one of the many horses that he has raised over the years, he also realizes that this is an animal far more untamed in spirit than he has ever encountered. Anyone can tell that this horse's soul is truly at unease.

With every desolate call and untamed cry made by the horse, Adam can tell that the sound is coming from a small clearing just up ahead. Holding his sword steadily in front of him for protection, he cautiously creeps in the direction from which he sounds came in order to investigate. He will not let the same trick fool him twice.

Ever so carefully, trying not to make one single solitary sound that would give his presence away, Adam slowly sneaks around some trees and edges his way along the ground. He is getting nearer to the sound of the horse. Advancing ever so slowly, he comes close to the edge of a riverbank, so that the water's edge is almost directly below him. Seeing a sudden movement in the near distance, Adam stops and tries to let his eyes adjust to the changing light.

The light cast off the river illuminates everything around the waters, keeping Adam somewhat hidden in the darkness surrounding them. Hearing the distressed horse crying once again, Adam can now see the troubled animal tied to a tree. The horse is only a couple of yards away from where Adam is hiding—it is Gispan's horse. Also below him, and slightly farther away, he sees the evil villain at the edge of the riverbank, gazing deep within its waters. Trying hard not to breathe, Adam watches closely to see what the wicked sorcerer is doing.

"Oh great *River of Reflection,*" Gispan speaks directly to the waters, "show me visions of the past, the present, and *especially* the future." The evil villain raises his staff over the water, slowly waving the wand back and forth, side to side. Intensely, he stares into the reflections created by the wand and his own image. He gazes deeply, waiting in eagerness for the waters to reveal their enchanted power and mysterious secrets. Undetected, Adam is also watching, wondering what it is that is happening.

Unlike Amiranda, who found it difficult to obtain a vision from the river, the mighty and evil Gispan has mastered the incredible powers and secrets held within the waterway. He knows how to call on them at his will, and how to use them to his benefit—for the good of all that is evil.

Adam inches closer, still careful not to be heard. Although he may not have the best view, he can still make out what it is that the villain sees.

Almost as clear as day, with the exception of the small waves rippling in the water, the river begins to share and unfold its hidden mysteries held within. First it shows the image of a violent whirlpool churning around in circles. A young woman falls off a cliff and into the waters, drawn and sucked into the raging waters below—it is Amiranda. Gispan also sees an image of himself as he is left standing at the edge of the cliff, laughing maniacally as she drowns a horrible and certain death. He is standing proud, tall, and strong, pleased by his sinful victory. Gispan smiles along with his own likeness. Suddenly that image is transformed.

Next, Adam can see the kingdom of Luxing. As Gispan is focusing on the watery image, he is still unaware that he is being watched. The depiction of the kingdom is current and everything is in its full glory, just as it is in the present day. The town is flourishing and happy, and all is lush and green. That image, however, will not remain unchanged for long.

Suddenly, a sprout begins to take root near the castle, peeking up from out of the grassy green meadow, which lies directly beside the princess' majestic and beautiful palace. Quickly, the sprout continues to grow taller and stronger, reaching high toward the sky. As it turns into a vine, similar to what Adam experienced himself only moments earlier, it envelops everything within its grasp. That vine quickly turns to two, next to four, then to sixteen, multiplying exponentially. They grow all around the castle and then throughout the kingdom. In an instant, the vines turn to shrubs, and then the shrubs change into trees. Ultimately the trees consume every inch of the land—leaving it all to wither, decline, and decay. It is all part of the wicked sorcerer's sinister plan, and it always was.

Witnessing the wicked plan, Adam realizes that he must do something to thwart the evil villain's plot. It is up to him to save the kingdom and help rescue the princess. But first, Adam knows that he must do something that will help him level the playing field. He just wonders if there is anything he can do.

While Gispan is still preoccupied with his plan, Adam takes a moment to himself to think. He wonders what would be the most effective way, and least dangerous way, given his position, to get at the evil villain. Adam wants to take this opportunity and use his advantage of surprise to aid him in his quest.

Besides the evil villain's mystical power, Gispan has two things to help him with his wickedness—his magic staff, which he is holding, and his mighty horse who is tied up only a few feet away from him, well within Adam's reach. Since Adam's own horse was taken from him, he thinks it to be a fair trade, at least for starters. After all, his sword may be mighty and powerful enough for vines and weeds, but the young rescuer will not dare to test its unknown strength on someone as powerful and as unpredictable as the evil villain. Not yet, anyway. It may not be much of a plan, but nevertheless, it is a plan.

The young man watches and inches up cautiously. Gispan is still entranced by the enchanted waters. By observing the steed and reading its behavior, Adam instinctually knows the horse will run for its freedom, if given the chance. For a moment he even considers riding him, in order to try to break the stallion, but he can clearly sense that this would be no easy feat, a daunting task by anyone's standards. Having grown up around horses all his life, Adam has never seen a horse as troubled as this one—in fact, no one has. Everything else considered, the best thing for him to do would be to set the animal free.

Having seen the image held within the river, the evil and mighty Gispan also realizes what he has to do. He must make sure Amiranda and the others are defeated. The shadowy figure stands, lifting his arms to the sky, holding his staff way up high—he is summoning some of his powers. This is Adam's chance to take the evil villain by surprise.

With one swift leap and a swing of his sword, Adam cuts the reins that secure Gispan's mighty horse to the tree, releasing him from Gispan's

control. Just then, the ground begins to tremble and shake—a result of Gispan's evil magic which he is using to thwart Amiranda and her friends. Gispan's black horse cries and neighs wildly, kicking up his front legs high into the air. Adam suddenly falls to the ground, a consequence of both the ground shaking and being taken off guard by the horse's reaction. Then, just as he predicted, the wild beast runs away, finally free of its evil master.

Gispan looks at all the commotion created by his horse, watching him as he runs away. It is just then that he sees Adam, finally free, still possessing the king's magical sword.

"If I can't have a horse in these woods, then neither can you," Adam tells him, almost mocking the wicked sorcerer. It is a foolhardy move, but still quite effective. The young man is on the ground but quickly picks himself up. Intelligently, just as fast as he appeared, he runs away, unwilling to face the evil sorcerer face-to-face.

Gispan is in awe. You can tell that he definitely did not see this coming. He was too busy looking into the future, but it was the present that was at stake. He is outraged by the feeble human—how the young man is able to be so bold and rash as to cleverly outwit him. Gispan will not make that mistake again.

With Adam disappearing into the woods, Gispan chooses not to go after him, as for now he has more important matters at hand—namely, Amiranda and her friends. Once again, he begins to call on his powers so that all who dwell in the forest would be in jeopardy.

Gispan begins to chant a wicked spell, as he wishes and dreams the words, which will somehow come true ...

The Wicked Plan

I see vines, I see weeds,
I see trees grow from seeds,
That crawl all along the ground.
I see fright and despair, everywhere;
I see nightfall all around.
And I know it will come to pass,
And I know I can make it last.

The kingdom will topple, their empire will fall,
And all of a sudden, I am ruler of all.
Out of the sunshine the blackness will crawl,
And there'll be darkness all around;
There'll be darkness all around.

Their world will grow colder, their bodies will shiver,
And the whole world around us will crumble and wither.
As destiny has it, it sure will deliver,
And I know it will come to pass;
And I know I can make it last.

The kingdom will topple, their empire will fall,
And all of a sudden, I am ruler of all.
Out of the sunshine the blackness will crawl,
And there'll be darkness all around;
There'll be darkness all around,
Here's to darkness all around.

Chapter 19

The Final Showdown

The ground continues to shake erratically, uprooting trees and shifting the ground beneath them as they run. Their presence there is definitely not wanted, as if someone or something wants them to give up and surrender to the deadly forest. It must be the mighty and evil Gispan causing such demolition and destruction, the princess thinks to herself. Someway, somehow, he must be stopped.

Unsteadily, Amiranda tries to maintain her footing as large rocks erupt from the earth below and tiny pebbles slip just beneath her feet.

Trees are falling every which way around them—narrowly missing the weary travelers as they run, dodge, duck, and cover from the cascading debris. Amiranda carries her pup, Peatie, in her arms, using her own body as a shield to protect him from any incoming danger. Miraculously, somehow they avoid being struck by the falling limbs as large branches and even trees continually fall all around them. The smell of smoke fills Amiranda's nose. Looking back, she sees the Deciduous Forest disintegrating into a wall of flame. Everyone runs frantically to stay ahead of the sheer devastation.

Amiranda cries to Jamarcus in desperation, "What are we going to do?"

"We have to rid Gispan of his magical staff and defeat him once and for all!" Jamarcus yells back, all too simply.

Jamarcus is starting to show a shortness of breath as he chooses to run ahead to lead everyone in the right direction. He stops time and time again to help keep the others safe from harm. To aid the others, he holds up tree branches so they can climb under, moves large tree trunks they otherwise would have to climb over, and assists them whenever they trip or falter. He makes sure no one gets left behind.

"Oh, *is that all?*" Sigmund replies, far from being satisfied with that answer. He knows that it would be near impossible to take Gispan's magical staff away from him, let alone defeat the powerful villain.

"Shut up, Sigmund, and run!" Simon retorts, attached to his unwilling counterpart. "We are connected, remember? I can't run faster than you!"

The two-headed turtle continues racing along the trail to keep up with the others. Although turtles are commonly known for being slow, Sigmund and Simon are racing turtles, so they manage to keep up for the most part. They also have a lot encouraging them to behave otherwise—

namely a huge wall of fire steadily closing in from behind and rows upon rows of falling trees toppling right beside them. Nevertheless, their heavy, armor-plated shell weighs them down from time to time, as the rest of the group pulls slightly ahead of them.

"Come on guys," Sherman says, running a few steps ahead of the rest. Once again displaying his keen leadership, he moves ahead to survey their path. This time, however, when he gives his command, he does it as a leader of a whole team.

"We are close to the forest's edge—we can make it! We can do it *together*," Sherman remarks, boosting everyone's morale for the moment. Well, that is *almost everyone....*

"Yeah, if we don't die first," Sigmund reluctantly declares as both he and Simon are still trying to do their best to keep up. Jamarcus picks them up and carries them for a while, relieving them for a bit. His wife runs slightly ahead of him, holding their child, and Amiranda is almost leading the pack.

Hastily they all run toward the clearing in the woodlands. The dwindling light from the start of dusk can be seen just atop the edge of the forest. Although not yet totally out of the woods, now the group can at least avoid being hit by falling trees. *What a relief,* the princess thinks to herself.

"We're almost in the clear," Jamarcus exclaims, running closer to the clearing. However, with the wall of flame encroaching from behind him and the darkness immediately in front of him, the Savant cannot track how far they have quickly traveled. Unbeknownst to him, the destination to which he is leading them is rapidly approaching.

Steadily, the swooshing sound of water can be heard in the near distance. However, it is evident to Amiranda that the sound is not that of a pond, a lake, a river, or even that of a waterfall, as she is far too familiar with all of these sounds. After all, she had just experienced all of these today, one right after the other. No, this sound was from something *far, far different.* It is a sound more intense, something almost frightening. Still, she is anxious to get to safety as everything behind them is being utterly destroyed. The burning forest is the last place anyone would want to be at a time like this. Amiranda runs up ahead, unaware that the trail on which she is running soon ends.

Jamarcus stops dead in his tracks. He holds his hand up high, waving his arm to caution the princess. "Amiranda, be careful!" he shouts. "Watch out! There's a—"

His warning comes too late, as Jamarcus cuts his own words short. Amiranda runs a bit too far, herself unaware of the steep hazardous cliff up ahead. The earth beneath her feet shifts as a rock is uprooted from the ground, caused by either the quaking earth or perhaps someone purposely causing it to happen. Either way, it must be the work of Gispan.

Unable to keep her footing, Amiranda trips and falls. She heads down the side of the bluff. As she falls, she somehow manages to toss Peatie to safety—throwing him up and over her shoulders. At the same time, she grabs to take hold of something, anything that will prevent her from falling. Everyone loses sight of her.

Peatie, who has succeeded at landing safely, is afraid to look. The young pup does not know where she is. He comes to the edge, careful not to fall himself. Peeking over the side of the cliff, he looks for Amiranda.

Miraculously, the princess has managed to take hold onto the edge of the cliff. Yet, she is still a few feet below the ledge. Amiranda holds on for her dear life, clinging and hanging onto one of the many sharp rocks that protrude out of the rock face. The rock is so sharp that it hurts and blisters her hands as she tries her best to hang on. She is unable to climb up to safety and no one is able to climb down to get to her. Here she remains helpless and all alone.

Looking beneath her, Amiranda quickly realizes what the swishing sound of the water was caused by. Below her is a raging whirlpool that is enormous in size. It swirls around and around in circles, swallowing everything that comes in its path. Surely if she were to fall, she would not survive the drop itself—not to mention the cold and raging waters circling below.

Peatie peeks a little farther over the edge, helpless as he looks down onto Amiranda and the near two hundred foot drop into the violent vortex. If he were to get any closer, he would fall himself. At just about that very same instant, Gispan magically appears. This time he is right in front of Jamarcus. As the evil villain stands there belligerently, he is also blocking the Savant from getting any closer to Amiranda. Cunningly and skillfully, he is preventing Jamarcus from helping the princess as she is about to plummet into the deadly waters.

Both men have no choice but to square off once again, more than likely for the last time, as there can be only one victor. This time, however, Jamarcus will not underestimate Gispan's sheer wicked and evil power. Here the two men stand, face-to-face, at the cliff's edge. As with Amiranda, both men are also overlooking the steep and deadly drop into the whirlpool below. For them, this is the final showdown.

Only a few yards away, Amiranda cries for help. She in not sure how much longer she will be able to hang on. She struggles hard to support herself, but no matter how hard she tries, the princess cannot pull her way up along the sharp rocks. The incline is too straight and too steep.

Unable to help her, Jamarcus has more immediate problems with which to contend. The mighty and evil Gispan is ready to end things for the Savant once and for all. The villain's mind is purely fixated on his adversary's defeat, and he is ready to do whatever it takes to conquer and vanquish him. For Jamarcus, saving Amiranda will have to wait.

"You are evil, Gispan," Jamarcus tells the villain as the two men circle one another relentlessly. Each one is ready to react in defense to the other's attack.

"You will refer to me as the 'Mighty and Evil Gispan,'" the villain retorts, seeking some respect in his self-given title.

Both are also ready to strike in offense, that is, if and when the time is right to do so. The look in each of the rival's eyes is extremely intense, as both are determined and dedicated to win. There is not going to be a second place here, just one ultimate winner. Both forces—one good, the other evil, are ready to face off and have their final battle.

The two opponents look one another over—first up, then down, then back up, staring into each other's eyes again. They are sizing each other up to see who will make the first daring and bold move.

"I have done nothing to you Gispan," the Savant retaliates, stating the truth. "I was not aware of your son's sacred burial ground."

Gispan's eyes widen. The innermost tips of his brows angle downward, making the shadowy villain appear even more vicious and evil. Gispan remembers the scene all too well, burying his son in the fields.

"It is not you that I am after," Gispan replies surprisingly. "I already avenged his death with you. You are nothing to me."

Jamarcus is shocked by Gispan's words. He is slowly starting to put all of the pieces together.

Meanwhile, Amiranda remains clinging to a small crevice in the side of the cliff. She holds on with only the tips of her fingers, with both her feet dangling freely below her. The princess cannot help but look below, petrified of falling into the vacuuming whirlpool. Making several attempts to regain her footing, she kicks her legs back and forth to try to grab a foothold in the rocks. Regrettably, the rocks only crumble and break loose as they slip away at her feet.

"Hold on Amiranda, don't look down!" Sherman's furry little face appears over the edge as he yells out to her. Amiranda's other animal friends also approach the edge of the cliff, trying to think of any way they can help.

Using his quick thinking and ingenuity, Sherman scurries up a nearby tree and chews off a piece of a long, thick, and heavy vine. Strategically he lets the vine fall right beside the other animals. They all carefully lower the line down to the princess to try to rescue her. Using their teeth, their claws, and their paws, the animals all brace themselves to the vine to hold it secure.

Even though each one of the animals is uniquely different, they all use their own special abilities to achieve the greater good. Skillfully, they all work in unison as a team.

Reynolds, at the very tail end of the vine, uses his beak to hold the line secure and flaps his wings to gain some additional thrust. Next in line are Sigmund and Simon—the two headed turtle. Both of them use their shell as an anchor to hold the vine close to the ground, and the edge of the cliff is used as a means of leverage and support. Sherman, standing just in front of them, uses his front paws to grab the vine, as his sharp teeth would surely slice right through it. Peatie is courageously up front, always remaining nearest to Amiranda. He takes hold of the vine using his teeth, clamping onto it with all his might. If anything, next to the princess, the small pup has the biggest chance of falling, being so close to the edge. Nevertheless, they all do not want to risk losing Amiranda to the dangerous peril.

For the moment, Amiranda's animal friends are able to successfully support her. However, their combined weight, strength, and endurance are not enough to pull her up, just merely hold her in place. Unable to maintain a firm grip on the vine, Amiranda is gradually slipping more and more toward the fierce whirlpool below.

Sherman gives the command for an old-fashioned "heave-ho." "Come on guys—*Pull!*" he orders. Still, Amiranda remains just out of reach and slipping.

Then, much to everyone's surprise, Sigmund offers his encouragement to the troubled young princess. "Hold on, Amiranda!" he yells out to her as he grips the vine ever so tightly. For once the self-absorbed turtle is showing that he is genuinely concerned for someone other than himself. Once more, they all give another firm tug on the vine, all using every ounce of strength to try to lift her up to safety. Still, despite all of their efforts, the princess continues to slip.

As all of Amiranda's animal friends try to save her from a certain demise, in the near distance they see Jamarcus and Gispan both ready to engage in battle. Although the mighty Gispan, as evil and powerful as he is, is far superior to the Savant in both his wickedness and his strength, he still knows better than to underestimate his enemy's ability.

Jamarcus, on the other hand, knows that he is overpowered and outranked. Still, he sees his family beside him, which gives him the courage, the strength, and the power to fight the evil villain. He remembers all the days, the months, and even the years of immense pain and sheer anguish when he was forced to live without the company of his warm and loving family. Jamarcus also recalls all the endless hours he toiled and stayed awake each night—searching to find the formula that would bring back his wife and son from the evil Gispan's pure wicked spell. It is quite ironic how the very same spell that for years bound his family in a solid pile of lifeless granite, also bound Jamarcus—binding him to a search to try to find a way to rescue them. This time, as the old saying goes, the Savant will "take no prisoners."

The Savant questions the villain. "If it is not me you want, then who is it you do want?"

Gispan pauses for a moment in reply. Taking his eyes off of Jamarcus, he looks down to where Amiranda is precariously hanging on for life.

"You scoundrel!" Jamarcus yells at the shadowy figure, realizing that it is Amiranda that he wants to put an end to. With her gone, Gispan will have all the power he needs—the power over the forest *and* over the kingdom. He is not about to let her go that easy.

Jamarcus charges the mighty and evil sorcerer, just like the time of long ago as told in Sherman's story. This time, however, Jamarcus is even more resolute and desperate to win. Clearly he has no other choice but to fight, as Gispan stands in the way of everything he has ever loved and cared about, and defeat is neither an option for him nor his family.

The two men engage, wrestling near the edge of the cliff, neither one clearly gaining a winning position over the other. Firmly locked arm in arm, they remain standing and fighting only a few yards away from the princess as she continues to slip down along the vine. Jamarcus hears Amiranda cry for help and, although unable to help her, he suddenly looks her way for a moment.

"Don't worry, I will save you!" Jamarcus cries out to her.

Although physically strong, the Savant's main weakness is the compassion he has toward others. The mighty and evil Gispan uses this to his advantage. At the very second that Jamarcus looks away, Gispan knocks him off of his feet, sending Jamarcus down to the firm ground. Jamarcus lies there motionless—literally only inches away from falling off the steep cliff.

"What are you going to do now—*Savant?*" Gispan mocks him. Clearly, there can be only one keeper of the forest.

With his back against the ground and his head hanging off the side of the cliff, Jamarcus struggles to get up but is unable to move. Gispan has him pinned down against the rock-hard soil, using all of his weight and power to restrain him. Having no other alternative, Jamarcus forces his aggressor to the side by rolling over, causing the evil sorcerer and himself to exchange positions. Both are up close to the precipice, so close that they are both about to fall over.

The two men alternate positions in battle, each one turning over—each one forcing the other into having their back hang over the cliff's edge. Their battle is almost like a choreographed dance, the way one man is attacking and the other defending, alternately. Small rocks tumble into the violent whirlpool below as the two men scuffle along the ground.

No matter how hard the two opponents try, neither one of them is able to outdo, overpower, or outmaneuver the other. By way of strength, power, and determination, Gispan and Jamarcus measure almost equally. It is a virtual standoff. In order for him to defeat the Savant, the evil sorcerer cannot win by brute force alone. Gispan knows he must resort to his supernatural abilities in order to end this battle permanently. The quicker it is done, the better.

With Amiranda still hanging precariously over the edge, and the Savant barely able to fight anymore, the mighty and evil Gispan magically begins to summon his powers. The villain's eyes glow fiercer and redder than ever witnessed by anyone before. The violent shaking of the ground beneath them in and of itself is enough to send everyone plummeting into the waiting whirlpool and to their doom, including the wicked sorcerer himself. This will surely send the Savant, Amiranda, and all of her animal friends right over the edge and down to their doom.

With all the earth in heavy upheaval, Jamarcus is nearly overcome by Gispan's mystical power. The intense shaking of the earth beneath him and the massive wind violently kicking back up again causes him to almost slip and fall.

Having no other alternative, strategically he tries to use this unexpected shift in motion to his advantage. In a final effort, he attempts to pull the mighty and evil Gispan up from off of him, and over the cliff's edge instead. His move is ineffective, as the evil sorcerer is far too powerful for his mere human tactics, no matter how clever or cunning they may be. With sheer delight, the evil sorcerer laughs at the human's feebleness.

"This is the end for you now, *Savant.*" Gispan mocks his silly little title once again, ready to stop these childish antics and tests of physical strength. He does not care in what manner Jamarcus is defeated, only that he cannot help save Amiranda. He stands up and reaches for his staff.

Jamarcus' wife's mouth gapes wide open as the evil Gispan is thrilled with his very own wickedness. Realizing that she is about to see her husband lose his life to the villain's wicked magic, she slowly turns her head from looking at the scene. She is unable to bear watching her own husband mercilessly defeated. The whole time she is protectively holding their crying baby in her tender arms, as he weeps and screams in fear.

Seeing his family's reaction, Jamarcus is suddenly overcome with a mixture of emotions—love, sorrow, helplessness, and pain. These uncontrollable emotions quickly turn into feelings of rage and fury toward the wicked sorcerer. He cannot forgive the sorcerer for bringing all of these past inflictions upon him and putting him in this state of turmoil. Clearly, the mighty and evil Gispan does not want, nor asks for, any forgiveness. This mixed confusion of contradicting sensations only fuels and infuriates the endeavoring hero all the more. Undoubtedly, Jamarcus must save himself for the sake of himself, his family, and his newly found friends.

In a focused, yet almost desperate fit of passion and fury, Jamarcus unexpectedly overcomes the evil villain's sheer dominance. With one swift and steady motion, Jamarcus uses every ounce of energy held deep within his heart and soul to bring the evil villain beneath him, plowing him firmly to the ground. Gispan is taken off guard by the Savant's sudden change of strength and will. Amiranda screams for help in the near distance, as she cannot bear to hang on much longer, and is now just about to let go.

Both struck hard by the blow, both men are unable to move. They both have had the wind knocked right out of them. In addition, they are physically exhausted, having fought as much as they possibly could. Jamarcus rests, his body perched on top of the villain, pinning him down. Both of their heads, and even part of their chests are hanging precariously over the side of the rock face.

Gispan, defenselessly pinned, turns his head to look for his staff. He was struck so hard by the blow that he barely even knows if it is still in his possession. With his eyes still refocusing, he sees his staff held tightly in his hand and his fist still clinched onto its shaft. Still, Jamarcus is holding both of his arms firmly against the hard, unyielding ground. The sorcerer is unable to move. The heartless villain realizes that he must call on not just some, but all of the power held within his evil scepter to win this final confrontation. To him, it does not matter if he lives or dies; the Savant must be defeated regardless of the consequences.

The evil sorcerer focuses, increasingly drawing all of his inner energies together to command the staff's supernatural energy. The magic sapphire begins to glow with a frail blue light, first glowing softly then growing more and more intense as it gains strength and power. The blue light becomes more and more blinding as the energy within builds up. The shadowy villain's eyes light up violently as he begins to summon all of his evil powers once and for all.

Just nearby, Amiranda is unable to hold any longer. Sherman also begins to give in, incapable of holding on as well.

"Amiranda, climb up!" the exhausted squirrel yells to her. "I—can't—hold—on—much—longer—!" he cries out. His voice is filled with exasperation; his words are broken due to his extreme shortness of breath. The other animals are about to give up as well, not being able to support her. They all grunt and groan as they tug on the rope that is securing her.

Amiranda shouts back, "I'm slipping!" She looks at the terrifying waters nearing below her. It is a losing battle for them as the princess keeps descending closer and closer toward the menacing whirlpool.

In the meantime, the glow of Gispan's magical staff is almost at full strength now. The villain's brutal eyes light up ferociously, as you can tell something wickedly evil is about to happen. In a last-ditch effort, he manages to pull the wand between him and the Savant. The staff is wedged between the two men, slightly separating them. The sorcerer knows that he has one, and only one chance to do this. The mighty and evil Gispan laughs maniacally as he is about to make his finishing move on the Savant.

At just that instant, Jamarcus, utilizing all of his will and strength, turns the evil Gispan on top of him. Simultaneously, he also rotates the villain's evil staff around, with the magical gemstone dangerously pointing toward its master instead of himself. Gispan's eyes widen, surprised by the unexpected switch in position. The evil sorcerer realizes that it is too late for him to stop the staff's mystical energies.

Without warning, the magical blue light funnels all of its power to its user instead, and both men are jolted by the wand's sheer and uncontainable might. The evil Gispan takes the brunt of the strike—with the force of the blow raising him almost vertically straight up into the air. Helplessly, he falls down into the center of the canyon, spinning powerlessly as he plummets directly into the cyclone of the turning whirlpool. Quickly, the whirlpool devours him, showing no mercy for the sorcerer's wicked soul. For the moment, all is quiet, and there is no trace of the evil villain.

The smell of smoke fills the air. No one knows what exactly happened, but for the moment it seems as though Gispan, the wicked sorcerer, has finally been defeated. Still, there is business that remains unsettled. The princess is still in danger and there is no one there who can help rescue her. That is, no one except for her small animal friends.

Chapter 20

The Rescue

Jamarcus lies motionless at the top of the rock face. The Savant is resting on his back, with the right half of his body lying precariously over the cliff's edge. In his right hand remains Gispan's magical and evil staff, which he is somehow left holding. There is still no sight of the wicked sorcerer—he has completely vanished.

With his right arm dangling unsteadily over the edge of the cliff, Jamarcus slowly releases the staff—either on purpose or by accident—it is unclear. He simply has no energy left in him to do otherwise. The rod falls for what seems like an eternity into the turbulent waters below. It too quickly vanishes as it submerges, drawn into the whirlpool just like its master only a few moments earlier.

"Jamarcus, are you alright?" the Savant's wife asks, concerned for his well-being. Still cradling their baby in her arms, she quickly runs to his side, now that it is safe to do so. For once their son has stopped crying, not feeling threatened by the danger. Meanwhile, Amiranda continues to hang on, but just barely.

The animals, still struggling to maintain a hold, are slowly losing their ground. They are fighting a losing battle, slipping nearer and nearer to the edge of the canyon. With the entire tiny amount of strength in their bodies that they can muster, they are determined to save the princess and not let her fall.

Sigmund pleads, "Hold on, Amiranda, hold on!"

Whereas before the animals were all spread farther apart holding the vine securely, they are now all huddled much closer together, right beside one another at the very edge of the cliff. In fact, they are dangerously near. They themselves are about to submit to the pressure of either letting go or falling into the whirlpool. For them, they simply have no other choice as they are out of options.

Just as the animals are about to slip and fall, a young man's arm reaches down for the vine. "Relax, I got you," says the rescuer. The stranger's arm slowly but surely pulls Amiranda to the top, grabbing onto her arm and wrist as she firmly grabs onto his. No one knows whose arm it is that grabbed her, but they realize that it is not Jamarcus, his wife, or anyone else that they know. The young princess is out of breath and faint-headed by now, but alas, she is finally safe.

Amiranda, like Jamarcus, now rests powerlessly on her back. The princess is staring vacantly up at the early evening sky, uncertain of her own surroundings. Torn, tousled, and disheveled from her narrow escape from death, she now appears all scraped up and scratched from the sharp rocks that she so desperately tried to ascend and cling on to. She looks far different from her usual prim and proper self—the typical vision of a royal and noble princess.

"I had no idea you were so beautiful," the young man's voice says as he stares, continuously looking upon the young lady. You can tell by the tone heard within his voice that his statement is truly genuine and his emotions are indeed authentic. "No one ever told me," the mysterious rescuer continues, holding her head up from the harsh ground. Still, Amiranda's eyes appear to be both bemused and bewildered as she still remains motionless and unable to speak.

Amiranda tries to focus and look at him, but for the moment everything still remains a blur to her. She attempts to regain her composure, but when she tests her own strength she is still unable to lift herself up. All the animals gather around the princess to see if she is all right.

"Your father sent me," the young man explains as he kneels beside the princess to comfort her. "He was so worried for you." Looking down upon her, the young rescuer gazes deep into Amiranda's delicate eyes, seeing how fragile she is.

"Just rest a minute, you had quite an ordeal," he tells her. Amiranda does not know what to make of her strange rescuer as she is still short of breath and doing her best to recover.

Slowly the young princess's eyes affix on the rescuer's image. Not only is she trying to figure out who he is, but she is also wondering what exactly just happened. Amiranda is still uncertain if Jamarcus and her animal friends are alright or not. She is even unsure if she is okay for that matter. While resting on her back and looking up, at first she sees only an outline of the gentleman's figure, as both her head and eyes are still quite fuzzy from the ordeal.

Little by little, she vaguely begins to see some of the features of her rescuer's face as they slowly come more and more into focus. First thing she notices is the brilliance of his smile and how radiantly it beams. Just from the look of it, Amiranda can easily tell that his smile is authentic. Next she sees a sparkle held within the young man's eyes. He has light blonde, flowing hair which is neatly trimmed at shoulder-length. Finally, she can make out the finer details of her rescuer's face. The young man is of average height, not too tall of stature, somewhat rugged, yet still very handsome.

It takes her a minute to absorb everything, but then finally at last, Amiranda regains her composure. She suddenly realizes what had just transpired. She sees Jamarcus with his wife and son, all the animals are alright and by her side, and thankfully there is no sign of the mighty and evil Gispan. She gently shakes the consciousness back into her head, dusting herself off at the same time.

"Are you alright, Jamarcus?" Amiranda asks as she pulls herself up along with her rescuer's help. He kindly pulls her to her feet before letting go.

"I'll be okay," claims Jamarcus, rising at the same time as Amiranda. He too brushes himself off, also much in disbelief over what just happened. His wife hugs him, holding herself steadfast to her husband; she clings to him almost endlessly. It is easy for everyone to see that she is incredibly thankful that he is all right. After a moment's embrace, Jamarcus approaches the strange rescuer.

"Thank you," the Savant says, pausing, waiting in response for the stranger's name. He holds out his hand to offer him a sign of peace.

The young man's eyes never leave Amiranda. "My name is Adam," the young rescuer replies as he kindly accepts Jamarcus' hand to shake. Although Adam's words are spoken to Jamarcus, his response is directed more toward the princess, as he is still gazing deep into her eyes. Amiranda smiles in return. At last, everyone is safe.

"And Gispan?" Amiranda asks, herself not having seen what happened.

"Don't worry, he's gone," Jamarcus replies. "Gispan and his evil staff are both gone."

Just then, and unexpectedly, the whirlpool's waters suddenly grow more turbulent as they begin to churn erratically. Something is terribly wrong; the wind begins to pick up and roar like thunder, echoing like cannons exploding throughout the canyon. The level of the water mysteriously starts to rise as the whirlpool becomes even more volatile and menacing than before Gispan fell into it. A tornado-like wind funnel begins to form—one nearly as wide as the canyon itself. The rocks on the side of the cliff begin to fall and everyone around is about to get sucked into the giant vortex created by the wind, the waves, and the water. The ground, previously steadied, is now violently shaking with enormous fervor. This time it feels as though the whole earth is going to explode from within.

Jamarcus, first appearing confused by the sudden eruption of events, swiftly realizes what it is that is happening. He remembers dropping the sorcerer's staff into the whirlpool, being unable or even unwilling to keep hold of it. Perhaps, he now thinks to himself, that was a mistake.

"Well Adam, it looks like we're not out of the woods yet," the Savant says. Although not intended, his words are taken quite figuratively, as in this case they take on a quite literal meaning.

Jamarcus' wife holds tightly to their son. "What's happening?" she asks.

Evidently, the encounter between the good Savant and the evil Gispan is not yet over as everyone originally thought. Amiranda and her friends appear even more worried than before, as each one fears the worst. Before, their enemy was clearly visible. This time however, he is unseen and, perhaps, even more powerful.

"Just what I didn't count on," Jamarcus explains. The Savant remains surprisingly calm, especially given the circumstances.

Amiranda, however, does not share that same composure. "What do we do now?" she questions, earnestly seeking a reply in return. Due to the noise created by the wind and the waves, she has to yell out her question to overcome their power and strength. The waters rise higher, growing more and more vicious. The wind also continually increases, and leaves blow all around them. The earth growls beneath their feet—and with each tremor, the ground breaks apart more and more. As big chunks begin to fall, the canyon starts to widen.

Sigmund reverts back to his spinelessness. "Is it time to run yet? That's the one thing I'm good at doing," he tells them.

"No!" they all reply in unison.

Not knowing what to do and not being able to run anywhere for cover, they all hold onto one another. Jamarcus offers up the only solution he can think of. Unfortunately for Amiranda, it is the one solution that is least imaginable for her.

"Amiranda," he tells her, "pour in the potion. It's our only hope!"

For a moment, Amiranda could not believe her own ears. The princess hesitates, seeking another solution. She holds the potion in her hand, thinking back to her sick Nana who so desperately needs the remedy. She also recalls the long journey she has been on and how long it took for her to get it. In her heart, she does not know if she can grant the Savant's request, even if it is the only way out.

"Can you make more?" Amiranda shouts back to him, trying to overpower the fierce, whistling winds and the surging currents which are rising steadily. The level of the turbulent water now climbs and nears the top of the cliff. The more it rises, the more it threatens to overflow and take everyone in with its current.

Jamarcus knows that another remedy would take months, even years, if one can ever be remade at all. It all would be too late by then. His laboratory has been destroyed, and along with it, all the potions, ingredients, and even the recipes needed to make more. Amiranda, being as bright and smart as she is, realizes the same.

"I don't know, but it's our only hope!" he shouts in reply, his eyes fixed on the waters that are now nearly reaching the brim of the canyon.

Sherman wishes for another alternative. "Is there any other way?" he asks, trying to compel the Savant into offering another solution. Again, it is not certain whether or not anyone can understand him, except for Amiranda, and the other animals of course.

Standing at the rock face's edge, Amiranda extends her arm over the side, holding the potion precariously over the edge. She slowly tilts the vial; she is unsure whether or not to pour it.

Adam, steadily holding the princess to ensure that she won't fall, softly asks her, "Is that the potion you have set out to find? The one to help save your Nana?

Unable to bear looking, she turns her head away from the vial. She buries her head deep in Adam's chest, her eyes protected from the wind and debris, thus blocking her view of the potion. She delicately whispers to him, "Yes" in reply, as she is about ready to pour out the liquid. The wind is practically pushing them into the whirlpool, as they hold on to each other for support. Large chunks of land break away from the sides of the cliff, endangering all who remain around the edge as well.

The princess knows that she must do what is best for the others. The others watch restlessly, holding onto each other for protection from the ill-fated wind as it gusts with sheer ferocity. Amiranda tilts the potion almost horizontally, with the liquid ready to spill.

Just as Amiranda is about to concede, Adam stops her.

"Wait, there's got to be a better way," he says as he tries to think of some other alternative. Although good-intentioned, his mind turns up blank, only furthering the inevitable.

The Savant, however, does not underestimate the untold power of his adversary. He knows that Gispan's evil power and strength has only grown stronger from his demise. "I don't think there is any other way!" he yells back, pleading to Amiranda to pour in the potion.

Then unexpectedly, the young rescuer pulls Amiranda's hand away from the edge of the cliff. With the potion still intact, the princess is prevented from giving in just yet.

"Let me try something," Adam quickly explains. The waters have now reached their brim and are starting to overflow around them, soaking their feet. The wind is howling violently through their ears and resounding through the canyon. Loose brush, debris, and leaves are circling all around them, almost piercing them like small projectiles. This may be the end for all of them.

Adam opens up his satchel and places his arm deep within. From one of his pouches he grabs a white powdery substance. He generously spreads the powder vigorously about, utilizing every last single bit of it. The tiny particles dissolve the very instant they hit the water. He holds onto Amiranda tightly, protecting her from the flying debris and wild hurricane-like winds.

For a moment, conditions initially worsen, with the belly of the earth churning in a deafening uproar. Trees shake as they bend and twist, and countless rocks, once deeply embedded steep within the cliff side, quickly surrender to the quake. It seems as though it is the end of the world.

"It's not enough!" the Savant yells as the churning waters begin to boil. Large bubbles form in the center of the whirlpool, and then quickly burst, releasing huge amounts of hot gas from within the earth's core. Everyone is clinging onto someone else in these last dark, tense-filled moments. Jamarcus holds on to his wife, Amiranda to Peatie and Adam, even Sigmund and Simon are both holding on to Sherman.

Seeing that his method is working, Adam thinks of the words spoken to him by the king before he set out on his quest. In his mind, the very same words repeat over and over. He realizes that he has only one other option....

With vigor, Adam pulls his sword from its sheath, holding it up high into the air. "Take this Gispan!" he announces as he throws the sword directly in the middle of the waters with great force. The shimmering sword quickly disappears, never to be seen again.

Then, to everyone's amazement, the circling waters begin to lose their momentum. The whirlpool gradually slows down, and the waters start to level out. The trees slowly stop swaying, and the dark clouds gradually disappear, showing the sun as it sets beyond the trees. Lastly, the waters recede, slowly retreating back to their original volume—deep down and far below, from well within the canyon. After a few moments, the once menacing tide quietly settles into a calm and gentle pond. At last, all is peaceful.

Jamarcus looks on amazed, stunned by the simplicity of the solution. "Now why didn't I think of that?" he says, realizing what it is that worked. Amiranda and everyone else just look at both men in awe, still wondering what just happened.

"Salt," Jamarcus replies simply. The Savant's response is very straightforward, yet at the same time he remains dumbfounded by the solution. Now finally revealed, the answer is so obvious to him, yet somehow was overlooked by him beforehand.

Amiranda is still perplexed by the strange occurrence. "I don't understand," she admits; she seeks some sort of explanation.

The Savant turns to her, looking as if he should have known what to do all along. "It cleanses" he replies. "Salt cleanses! The sword was made from the salt of the earth," he affirms.

Jamarcus then turns to Adam once again. "Good work, my friend," he tells him, praising the rescuer's efforts as he offers to shake his hand yet another time. Adam graciously accepts.

Everyone is overcome with joy, happy that everything has finally returned to normal. The animals celebrate among themselves, dancing and chanting in victory. Jamarcus is also filled with delight. He is happy to be alive and with his family, and to know that Amiranda has the potion her Nana so desperately needs. Finally, he realizes that it was the salt held within his loving tears that freed his family from Gispan's wicked spell. It was also salt that ultimately defeated the evil villain himself.

Adam modestly replies, "It was just a lucky guess."

They all hug and embrace one another as they rejoice in their incredible accomplishments. Working together they have found the potion Amiranda needs, defeated the evil sorcerer, and restored peace to the forest. Jamarcus gives Adam a hug, patting him firmly on his back, and then messing up his hair with the palm of his hand. To Amiranda, the display of affection is quite amusing, as it reminds her of a father who is truly proud of his son, openly showing his gratitude.

The two men chuckle, together side by side and arm in arm, as they turn and walk away from the edge of the cliff. Everyone else joins in with their laughter.

Lastly, Jamarcus puts his arm around Amiranda. He gently tugs on her shoulder, pulling her closer to him. Humbly, he tells her, "Now Amiranda, why don't we all get you home."

Amiranda is thrilled to finally hear these very words. Her face lights up; she is ready to go home. She cannot wait to tell her Nana of all her adventures, and give her the cure that she needs. They all gleam with delight. That is at least, almost all of them.

Somehow, Simon seems a little downcast. The expression on the small turtle's face is filled with sorrow and regret. He interrupts the celebration. "Amiranda," he says, all choked up, "we can't leave the woods." He looks down to the ground below, reminding the others that this is their home.

"What?" she asks. Amiranda kneels down to her new friend, confused and saddened by his sorrowful reply.

Sherman confirms the unfortunate truth in his statement. "Yes, this is true," the squirrel explains. "You see Amiranda, *this is our home;* this is where *our* family is."

A time of jubilation suddenly becomes a time for departure amongst close friends. Although joyous seconds earlier, everyone is saddened to have to say good-bye.

"But you can't leave me," Amiranda insists. She pauses. "Not after we've come so far." The princess' eyes start to water as she holds back the tears.

"We'll always be with you," Simon reassures her. The turtle smiles at Amiranda. He is clearly happy to have her as a friend and he obviously will always cherish their memories together.

Just then, Sigmund surprisingly offers a valuable reminder to Amiranda and the others. "Amiranda," he tells her sincerely, "remember when Gordy said 'Family—now that's important'?"

The princess smiles; she already realizes his point.

"Well, truth is you've been like family to me, and I will never forget you for that."

For the first time in his life, the continually irreverent and always uncompassionate turtle is warmhearted and wells up with emotion. Sigmund has clearly made a huge change in personality, perseverance, and attitude. In fact, every one of them has grown in character along this journey. "Now I figure I'd better go off to be with my family," he tells them, all teary-eyed.

"I think I understand now," Amiranda affirms. The princess thinks about her own family and how things could be different, perhaps if she tried a little harder. It is a tearful moment for all as they bid one another a fond farewell.

"Thank you friends, good-bye!" Jamarcus tells the animals. He pets Simon and Sigmund, rubbing each on the head, much the same as he did with Adam moments before. He then stands at attention and salutes Sherman for his courage, bravery, and leadership. The squirrel returns the salute with his paw raised firmly to his brow.

Reynolds squawks, "Good-bye! Warrk, good-bye." He spreads out one wing, waving to them.

Finally, it is Amiranda's turn to bid farewell to her new friends. In her heart, she knows that it is impossible for her to express the love and gratitude she feels towards them. She also knows there is nothing she could possibly say to them that would rightfully praise them for the kindness and effort they have shown throughout her journey. Good-byes are tough, and like Simon says, they will always be together in one way or another, not only in mind, but also in spirit as well as in heart.

She curtsies before them, a respectful gesture of her nobility. "You are all so wonderful," she tells them, kneeling humbly at their feet. "Thank you—"

She pauses for a moment, taking time to choose the exact words she would like to say. She wants to choose the words that would best describe each of them individually, yet still sum up the group together as a whole.

Amiranda starts with Sherman, who is standing closest to her and slightly in front of the others. Looking directly at him, she says, "Thank you for your bravery and leadership." She bows her head appreciatively and then kisses him lightly on the cheek. The flattered squirrel blushes in return, honored to be commended for his heroics. He is somewhat flushed with embarrassment by her words, but much more so by being kissed by a girl as beautiful as she, nonetheless a princess.

The princess then turns to Sigmund, the known cynic of the group. She smiles at him kindly, knowing that the two of them have grown so much over the course of the journey.

She continues by commending him, "Thank you for your courage and strength." Amiranda thinks back to all the times Sigmund put his own safety at risk, not only for her sake but also for her friends' sake. She bows her head graciously and kisses him on his cheek, just like she did to Sherman. Sigmund turns slightly red with embarrassment as well. He remembers how at first he did not want anything to do with the young girl and her friends, and now he wishes that they did not have to part. His eyes well up with tears, which is very unusual for him, as callous and cold-hearted as he is used to behaving.

Last but not least, Amiranda turns to Simon, her most welcoming and helpful animal companion in the forest. Without Simon's unwavering commitment, Amiranda knows she would never have gotten the help she needed to make it through the forest alone.

The princess continues, "and thank you for your friendship." Although teary-eyed, she always maintains her dignity and poise as a princess.

With their good-byes all said, Jamarcus finally turns to Adam. "You will take care of Amiranda and show her the way home, right?"

Amiranda is surprised by the Savant's words. She knows that the animals must stay, but as for Jamarcus and his family, there is simply nothing left for them here.

"Aren't you coming back to Luxing? We've got plenty of room at the castle," Amiranda kindly offers.

Jamarcus' reply is simple, yet effective. "My home is here, in the forest, with my family and with the animals. You see, to me this is my castle."

The Savant looks at Adam, seeking a response to his question that he will take care of them from here on. Adam nods his head as he firmly shakes the Savant's hand one last time. "It has been a pleasure," he tells him. "No problem, I will lead them home," he answers.

"No problem, Warrk! No problem," Reynolds agreeably repeats. He flies around and lands on Adam's shoulder, showing his trust in his new friend. They all giggle and laugh.

The two groups wave good-bye to each other as Amiranda, Peatie, Adam, and Reynolds proceed on the trail back home. They all make their way down the path that heads back to the castle. Slowly they fade into the distance and disappear over the hill as the setting sun also fades and disappears along with them.

P

Chapter 21

Back Home

Days went by and years had passed. Outside Amiranda's great big bedroom window, it is the dawn of spring. The pond beneath her window is vibrant and alive, bursting and teeming with life. Frogs leap from lily pad to lily pad, and now instead of one lonely butterfly seeking to find its solitary way, there are many families of butterflies filling the air. The once dark and desolate Deciduous Forest is now green and lush. Even the town of Luxing is flourishing, and its buildings are growing taller and becoming more plentiful in number.

Amiranda's hand pushes the window open, letting in the fresh spring air. Her old bedroom is now beautifully redecorated as a nursery, which is freshly painted a baby blue color and a small baby's cries are heard. Beside the window, there is a white bassinette with a white lace canopy on top.

Inside the crib, a newborn infant lies restless. He is tiny and cute, with a nose that displays small, dainty ripples whenever he laughs or cries. Amiranda is several years older now; she picks up the child, placing the baby in her arms—it is *her* baby. Adam is standing by her side, smiling at the two of them—his loving wife and their newborn son.

"Look at him," Amiranda tells him; "he's going to be a *real* prince." The both of them giggle over Amiranda's play on words. They are overjoyed with the new addition to their family. Almost at the exact instant that his mother picks him up, the baby stops crying and begins to laugh and smile. It is easy to see that he is very happy to be held, and Amiranda is more than happy to oblige, just like the way she always used to hold Peatie when he was a small pup. Amiranda cradles her newborn son in her arms, rocking him gently back and forth and smiling radiantly the whole while.

Peatie's yelp is heard at their feet, playfully seeking some attention from Amiranda and his new co-master, Adam. He is full grown now, about four to five times the size he used to be as a pup. Peatie jumps up to Amiranda, careful not to disturb the baby, and begs her to pet him. He rubs his head against her hand for comfort, while holding a ball in his mouth, eager to play and drooling all over it.

"Oh Peatie, don't be jealous," Amiranda tells him. "You know I love you just as much," she giggles.

Adam ruffles the fur on the top of Peatie's head, much in the same manner as Jamarcus had done to him years earlier, proud to have him as a faithful companion. Peatie jumps up and licks his face in return.

"Come on, Peatie," Adam cheerfully tells him, "little Baby Andrew can't play ball yet. I'll take you out in a minute—I promise." Peatie jumps around in circles and pants eagerly in response, at the same time wagging his tail enthusiastically. It makes a loud thumping sound as it repeatedly hits one of the crib's legs.

Their camaraderie is briefly interrupted by a womanly voice heard at the door. "I thought I heard my precious angel," the elderly woman says. It is *Nana's voice* that is heard outside the room. Although the door is already partway open, she respectfully knocks before entering.

"Come on in, Nana," Amiranda tells her affectionately.

Letting herself in, Nana is looking much more youthful and vibrant in appearance than she ever did. "I did hear my little angel!" she replies, answering her own question. "Can I hold him for a moment?" she asks, motioning to Amiranda by putting out her arms to hold the baby.

Amiranda gently places the baby in her arms. "Sure Nana," she tells her, "here you go." Nana takes baby Andrew and sits down and cradles him in the rocking chair, softly swaying him back and forth. She calms the baby down in the same way she used to do to Amiranda when she was an infant. Amiranda glows radiantly with delight.

Now fully open, a succession of three quick, soft knocks is heard at the door. Amiranda's parents stand in the doorway, the king and queen. Both King Jedrek and his wife, Queen Isabel, are smiling joyfully, almost grinning from ear to ear. The queen chimes in happily, "Oh how's my little one?" She raises her voice whimsically, in the playful manner grown-ups tend to make toward sweet little babies.

Adam replies, "He's cute as a button." Affectionately he reaches out and touches the tip of the baby's nose. The size of his index finger shows just how small and tiny the infant really is.

"Takes after his grandfather," King Jedrek interjects proudly. He is clearly kidding his new son-in-law, taking the credit for the child's good looks. He smiles at Amiranda and the baby giggles as if responding to his joke. "Has a good sense of humor too—just like his granddad," he chuckles jovially. The rest join in with laughter. At last, everyone is together and behaving like one big happy and loving family, or at least, that is *almost everyone* is together.

Adam looks around the room, noticing someone missing. "Amiranda," he asks, "where's Reynolds?"

Before Amiranda even has the chance to answer, Reynolds suddenly swoops in from outside. Swiftly he flies around the room and perches himself on the windowsill with grace. Even Reynolds has learned a thing or two over the past few years.

"Hello! Warrk, hello," Reynolds squawks. Right behind him flies in another parrot, only smaller with greener feathers—a female. She lands right next to him and cuddles and coos beside him.

Amiranda points to the two parrots as they nuzzle together. "Hey, look everyone—*Reynolds is in love!*" she professes. Everyone giggles and laughs.

Amiranda's mom joins in the humor. "Alright guys, we'd better leave the lovebirds alone—*all four of them,*" she says jokingly. Once again, they all chuckle in amusement.

"Amiranda," Queen Isabel continues, "what time are Jamarcus and his family coming over for dinner? You know I'm cooking myself. Kistoffe has been showing me how."

"Promptly at six," Amiranda politely replies. "And be sure not to get pepper everywhere like Kistoffe, it makes my nose tingle!" Amiranda twitches her nose, displaying the dainty ripples.

They all laugh, and Amiranda's parents exit the room. Nana hands the baby back over to Amiranda, then hugs the princess with one hand around her shoulder while running the other hand through baby Andrew's hair. She then leaves as well.

Reynolds and his new love, ready to start a family of their own, also exit but they fly out the window instead. Flying together side by side and wing to wing, the two head directly toward the fresh spring meadows. They both sail off into the sunset.

Finally, Adam and his wife are alone with their newborn son, with Peatie still sitting ever faithfully by their side. Amiranda remembers the time when she was always protecting him as a small pup; now it is Peatie who sits there vigilantly on watch—always guarding and protecting her and her baby. He lies down at Amiranda's feet, always staying as close to her as he possibly can.

Adam and Amiranda stare and gaze at their baby Andrew with delight, and then Adam gives his wife a tender kiss on the cheek. He then tells Peatie, "Come on boy—let's go play ball." Peatie jumps up as quick as quick can be, and the two exit the room playfully to go have some fun outside. At last, all is peaceful and quiet.

Both alone now, Amiranda looks at her newborn son dearly, thankful to have a life as wonderful as she has had. She gently walks with him to the window, cradling him in her arms, softly swaying him to sleep. The setting sun lights her face, further enhancing her already glowing countenance—as her happiness inside cannot be hidden. She stares out the same window that she stared out of so many times; when she herself was growing up.

As she cradles her baby, she thinks about so many things—her life as a

child, her journey through the forest and the friends she made there, and the will inside her that always kept her striving and wanting something more. Finally, she realizes that everything she had ever wanted was right inside this castle's solid and hard stone walls all along; she just had to travel far in order to find it.

She gazes out the window, watching the two playful parrots fly lovingly around one another. She sees the once dark and desolate Deciduous Forest now green, fervent, and alive. She sees Adam tossing the ball to Peatie, and Peatie happily retrieving it. Lastly, she smiles at her son Andrew and he smiles back at her. Everything is absolutely perfect and happy with her world.

As the setting sun slowly sets, the end of the day's light casts a distinct silhouette of Amiranda holding her newborn baby. The two of them are neatly centered in the window, both overlooking the vast world over which they will one day reign. She is so thankful to have had the life that was set out for her—a life she was truly destined to fulfill. The princess thinks to herself, "This must be what life is all about."

Amiranda never did get her wings, but surely she did get to fly. Softly she sings to herself and her newborn baby …

If I Could Fly,
I'd surely have wings;
I'd rise to the top
Of everything
-If I Could Fly
-If I Could Fly.

~THE END~

List of Characters

(In alphabetical order)

Adam: The young man sent by Amiranda's father (the king) to help try to save the young princess. Adam has many hero-like qualities and is kindhearted and very gentlemanly, always ready to lend a hand. Adam sets on a quest to find Amiranda, who is on her own quest, in the mysterious and dark Deciduous Forest.

Amiranda: The main character of the tale, a young princess who is determined to find something more to life than what is within her castle's solid walls. Amiranda is cute and childlike in the beginning, especially with everyone around trying to keep her that way, but as her journey grows, so does Amiranda.

Claws: The vicious leader of the spider crabs which have taken over part of the "River of Reflection." He leads his army in the great "River Battle," a battle that takes place between his spider crabs and Amiranda's river friends, the blowfish and the Japanese fighting fish.

Doc: The royal family's doctor, who oversees the medical needs of Amiranda and her noble family. Like any medical doctor, there are certain things that he simply cannot cure, which leads Amiranda on a quest to help save her Nana.

Gispan: The mighty and evil sorcerer who reigns over the Deciduous Forest. He has a dark, shadowy figure and his eyes glow a mysterious fiery red whenever angered. Gispan rides a black, angry stallion that appears and disappears with him in the forest.

Gordy: The ringleader of the blowfish gang, who come to help save Amiranda from the vicious spider crabs. Riley, Stiley, and Trent are Gordy's three main club members. Gordy teaches Amiranda how important family can be.

Jamarcus: Also known as the *"Savant,"* the mysterious alchemist who lives in the forest. He is incessantly trying to find a way to undo Gispan's evil magic that overtook the forest and his family. Jamarcus' wife and son were both turned to stone by the mighty and evil Gispan because he unknowingly built his home on the sorcerer's land. Jamarcus desperately seeks a way to bring his family back to life—but first, to do so, he must defeat Gispan.

Jove: Princess Amiranda's astute butler, assigned to attend to her needs and oversee her formal upbringing. Jove is very keen to goings-on in the castle, yet he still chooses to remain detached from what happens there.

King Jedrek: Amiranda's father, the noble and royal king of Luxing. The king is very stern and strict; he rules his kingdom with efficiency. Having no time for Amiranda himself, he has his hired assistants help care for her.

Kistoffe: Princess Amiranda's personal chef who is overly French, or how he says, *"Franch."* Kistoffe is very fond of the princess, and she shares her own dreams and desires with Kistoffe, dreams which the French chef could never possibly fulfill.

Molly: Amiranda's pet goldfish. Molly remains alone in her oversized tank, only able to look at the outside world from the tank in which she lives. In many ways, Amiranda is just like her pet goldfish; lonely, isolated, and confined to the place they live.

Nana: Amiranda's caregiver. Even though she is of no real family relation to Amiranda, she is the closest to the young princess emotionally, and Amiranda considers her to be like her very own grandmother.

Peatie: Amiranda's best friend, a small, timid, and young puppy who trails the young princess every step of the way. Peatie is affectionate, cute, cuddly, and loyal to Amiranda; he is like any good pup should be.

Queen Isabel: Amiranda's mother, the queen of Luxing. Because Amiranda has a formal caregiver, her Nana, the young princess really does not have much interaction with her own real mother, especially as she grows up.

Reynolds: Amiranda's colorful pet parrot, a parrot that mimics everyone with his whimsical sayings. As Amiranda's second pet, he is always vying for attention and at sorts with her other pet, Peatie.

Roxen: An unemployed court jester who is continually trying to get work at the castle. Roxen is overzealous in his antics and basically a blundering fool when it comes to entertaining the king.

Sherman: The squirrel that Amiranda meets in the forest, who always shows dedication, military prowess, and is a natural-born leader. Like any leader, Sherman makes mistakes, which he must continually overcome.

Shiro: The kind and wise leader of the Japanese fighting fish group known as the "Samurais." He leads the other Japanese Beta fish into the famous "River Battle" of the forest. Although his eyesight is lacking, by no means does that detract from his expert fighting abilities.

Sigmund and Simon: The two-headed turtle who has split personalities, thereby constantly creating conflict between the two. Simon is the nicer, more pleasant mannered turtle, whereas Sigmund is self-centered, despondent, and aloof, and always thinking of himself first.

Whitetail: Adam's faithful, trusted, and loyal horse. Raised by Adam since she was a foal, she helps lead Adam into the forest where they both face the dangers held within its deep, dark, and mysterious boundaries.

Yule: King Jedrek's royal guard. He is rather clumsy and awkward, dressed in full body armor that he simply cannot get used to wearing. Being that the kingdom of Luxing is a peaceful kingdom, there is no genuine need for him, but every king of high importance has to have someone stand guard.

List of Songs

(In performance order)

About the Author

JOHN ADAMO is a Long Island-based author and songwriter who has copyrighted more than four hundred poems and has both written and composed numerous songs and short stories. Music has always been an integral part of John's life, as he has performed at different venues all across Long Island—both as a professional pianist since the age of seventeen (one year after his father passed away) and also as a disc jockey/emcee for various private parties and public events.

This is John's first formal work, which was originally written as a screenplay and copyrighted in 1998. John has always had the visualization that an animated movie would one day be made from his work. The author wanted to put together a story unlike any other, and one that could be enjoyed by people of all ages … both young and old alike. A story that reinforced good values, covered common ethics, and taught morals as John feels those important criteria are so often left out in today's modern fairy tales.

After having the screenplay sit on his shelf for nearly fifteen years, John felt that it was finally time to let the world know the life and world of Amiranda—a Cinderella-type princess who has everything in the world that a princess could possibly ask for, but is still missing something more in her life. Through your reading, John hopes that Amiranda's dreams of living will virtually be realized. Last but not least, John hopes you like Amiranda's story just as much as he enjoyed writing it … Enjoy!

AMIRANDA

Princess Amiranda and the Tale of the Deciduous Forest

For more information regarding John P. Adamo and his work, visit his website: www.princessamiranda.com

Additional copies of this book may be purchased online from www.LegworkTeam.com; www.Amazon.com; www.BarnesandNoble.com; or via the author's website: www.princessamiranda.com

You can also obtain a copy of the book by visiting
L.I. Books Bookstore
80 Davids Drive, Suite One, Hauppauge, NY 11788
or by ordering it from your favorite bookstore.

CPSIA information can be obtained at www.ICGtesting.com
Printed in the USA
BVOW022204140512

290175BV00001B/12/P